WET DREAMS ON LOCKDOWN

The Warden

SHAWNICE

URBAN AINT DEAD

ISBN: 979-8-9902387-5-6

CONTENTS

SOUNDTRACKS

Scan the QR Code below to listen to the Soundtracks/Singles
of some of your favorite U.A.D titles:

Don't have Spotify or Apple Music?
No Sweat!
Visit your choice streaming platform and search URBAN
AINT DEAD.

Currently on lock serving a bid?
JPay, iHeartRadio, WHATEVER!
We got you covered.

Simply log into your facility's kiosk or tablet, go to music and
search URBAN AINT DEAD.

SUBMISSIONS

Submit the first three chapters of your completed manuscript to urbanaintdead@gmail.com, subject line: Your book's title. The manuscript must be in a .doc file and sent as an attachment. The document should be in Times New Roman, double-spaced, and in size 12 font. Also, provide your synopsis and full contact information. If sending multiple submissions, they must each be in a separate email. Have a story but no way to submit it electronically? You can still submit to URBAN AINT DEAD. Send in the first three chapters, written or typed, of your completed manuscript to:

URBAN AINT DEAD
P.O Box 448
Maybrook, NY 12543

DO NOT send original manuscript. Must be a duplicate.
Provide your synopsis and a cover letter containing your full contact information.
Thanks for considering URBAN AINT DEAD.

Chapter 1

inwood Michael's, the Warden at Belmont Women's Correctional watched the thick light skinned woman with long box braids on his flat screen as he lounged on his black leather sofa in his office, a cigar in one hand, in the other a jack and coke, gasping every few moments as the wet mouth of one of his prisoners slurped and sucked his large member.

"Shanea Rollins, a jury of your peers have found you guilty of armed robbery in the 2nd degree," the judge on television said.

A jury of her peers…not in the slightest. She scanned the faces of the twelve people who had signed her sentence. Five older white men with Windsor ties and jackets, six older white women in church dresses, and a woman who Shanea wasn't even sure spoke English. *That* was supposed to be the jury of her peers.

She rolled her eyes and then looked back at the judge. "Because of your refusal to tell the court who else perpetrated this crime with you, I have no choice but to levy the maximum sentence." He paused and the room went deadly silent. "I hereby sentence you to no less than twenty years at Belmont Women's Correctional."

Shanea smirked and the judge asked, "Do you wish to say anything to the court?"

Shanea sung along with the $tupid Young's beat in her head.

Catch a case, don't snitch, that's mando (that's mando)
Ride for your clique, that's mando (that's mando)
Broke, hit a lick, that's mando (that's mando)
Always with the shits, that's mando (that's mando)

Shanea stared through the judge and smiled, "We don't snitch at Wild Beat Studios, that's mando. I was there alone."

Linwood grinned as the crowd gasped when she said it. He liked her feisty spirit…he would need to break her. He placed his glass on the end table beside him and moved his hand onto the woman's head who was kneeling in front of him.

"Suck…harder," he growled, patting her on her cornrows.

He thrust up as he shoved the prisoner's head down, his palm twisting on her large cornrows, the sound of her gagging making his member pulsate as her spit rolled down the shaft as she reached the base.

Soon it would be Shanea Rollins kneeling between his legs, trying to get time off the sentence she just received like this one was. No one ever got time off, but he would tell his prisoners anything to get the head he liked. His wife's head game was horrible at best.

He watched Shanea turn in her orange prison jumpsuit, his "O" face coming and going from the throating as the sheriff placed the shackles on her wrists and led her toward the exit, her large ass hugging the fabric. He licked his lips as she left the courtroom to the constant click of the cameras. The door Shanea walked through opened and then closed as Linwood's breathing heightened. He felt his balls constrict.

"That's it," he groaned. "Get that sentence cut—-" Linwood's jaw dropped and his eyes opened wide as he released, holding the woman's head down as she choked on it.

"Whew…fuck…," he shouted as his hips shimmied.

With a final groan, he let the kicking prisoner loose and she fell back on her ass on his Persian rug. The nut dripped from her bottom lip as she wiped it with the back of her forearm, then coughed. Linwood rolled his neck over the edge of the couch with a sigh.

"Aisha, you have the best throat in Belmont," he moaned as he blinked. "You can go now."

Aisha stood up and wiped her mouth one last time and then walked to the door, opened it, and walked through, leaving an emptied warden who clicked the remote on the TV to shut it off and leaned his head further over the edge of the couch for a nap. He had to rest up for the celebrity rapper they called Lady Blaze. But to the prison's registry, she was Shanea Rollins, the most famous guest of the state.

"BITCH, if you don't move, I'ma beat yo ass," said the overweight dark-skin skank behind Shanea who was waiting to get on the bus to Belmont.

Shanea ignored the comment until she felt a bump in her lower back. "Hear me famous ho?"

Shanea rolled her eyes and then turned her head to both sides to check the guard's distance from her place in line. She knew what would happen to her when she did what she was about to, but you can never be a punk in prison…never, no matter the penalty for the chin check.

Shanea stumbled a few inches from the next bump. "I'ma have fun making you my bitch," the woman snarled. "You fittin' to keep my commissary full."

Shanea shook her head with a smirk, then tapped her foot and slowly turned her top half so as not to let the guards know she was going to make her move until the last moment. The woman made eye contact and Shanea smiled.

The other woman sneered, her gold tooth stark against her otherwise perfectly white teeth. "Sup, then bitch," the woman snarled. "Ready to be my clit sucking whore?"

Shanea didn't even hesitate. She spun completely around,

reared her head back, box braids swaying across her back, and brought it crashing down on the woman's upper lip, just under her nose making blood splash across her face as the other prisoners cheered around them. The woman cried out as she dropped to her knees holding her bleeding mouth, the gold cap clattering on the concrete between them along with her two front teeth.

"Sup then," Shanea shouted before falling to the ground as the guard's billy club hit her lower back and thighs, sending her to her knees.

Thwack…thwack…thwack.

Shanea growled in pain and spat on the ground before biting her lip as she held her breath to stop crying out. One blow, another blow, and as she braced herself for the third and fourth blow, she heard someone roar, "Stop!"

Hearing the voice, Shanea cut her eyes and exhaled a deep breath between pursed lips, breathing in shakily as she tried to stop the searing pain coursing through her lower back. She wouldn't give the pigs the pleasure. Shanea blinked the tears away as the other prisoner lay moaning in front of her, blood dripping from her mouth.

Shanea watched the older woman with dark skin and a shaved scalp approach, her black shoes shined to a high sheen in her crisp grey uniform. She towered over Shanea and glared down at her. "Just cause you're famous, don't mean you can get rowdy without punishment," she hissed. "On your feet, convict."

Shanea coughed, pressed her palms to the concrete, and pushed herself up. She made it to her feet and turned to face the lieutenant. The women stared at one another for a long moment, and then the lieutenant brought her baton to her nameplate over her flat chest and tapped it. "My name is Lieutenant Gibbs, understand?"

Shanea nodded then winced. "Yeah."

"Good," she said. "Now get your dumb ass on the bus, convict."

Shanea turned around as the other COs started moving the prisoners past her. She felt Gibbs' eyes glued to her ass. As the last prisoner passed her, Shanea glanced over her shoulder and the pair made eye contact again. Shanea smirked and gave a knowing nod to Gibbs who gave a slight lick of her lips before walking back to her patrol car parked behind the bus.

If she had a nickel for every woman and man who stared at her perfect round apple ass, she would have been a millionaire without rapping. She was already but that was from hard work, not what God gave her. She didn't shake ass for money anymore, but it paid the bills until her career went through the roof.

Shanea glanced at the blood and gold cap on the concrete as one of the COs snatched the woman off the pavement and then walked her back inside the jail for medical treatment.

The other woman sneered at Shanea and mouthed, "Be seeing you."

Shanea laughed as she turned back around and got on the

bus. When she stood next to the driver, one of the officers, a blond woman with spiked hair and a massive chest, shoved her into the first row. Shanea landed and winced as her back made contact with the side of the bus.

"Have a seat convict," the guard said.

Shanea cleared her throat and stared out the window for the long bus ride to Belmont Prison._The bus ride was uneventful as they disappeared from civilization.

Shanea stared at Belmont Prison as it came into view as the sun set over the walls, its giant guard towers looming over the bus, seemingly blocking out what part of the sun remained.

The drab reinforced concrete walls went twenty feet in the air and had guards strolling the walkways. Their backs were to her as they stared down inside the prison yard, rifles at the ready. Belmont was known to be the most violent prison in the state. And more than one prisoner had died as a result of the understaffing.

Shanea swallowed the lump in her throat as her heart thumped in her chest and the adrenaline coursed through her veins. The closer to the gate, the harder her heart thumped. As they approached the gate, the bus came to a slow stop with screeching brakes. Shanea winced when she heard the sound that was worse than nails on a chalkboard.

"Prisoner Rollins, you will be the last off the bus," the blond guard said, rising to her feet.

Shanea turned her head. "Why?" she growled.

"Lieutenant is walking you in for the search. You're

important," she said with an eye roll as she air-quoted the word. "Now, shut the fuck up."

The blonde turned and addressed the prisoners. "Okay, trash. You will file out of this bus and walk single file into processing. Now, stand up."

The other prisoners stood up and started to file out of the bus as the guard led the way, the bus driver right behind her. Shanea watched each of them pass and stare at her. For many of them, it was their first time even seeing a celebrity, and probably their last with the sentences usually handed down at Belmont. Shanea was used to it by now, but she knew she would be targeted immediately when she got in the pod. And she also knew isolation was going to be her constant companion for the next two decades. She wasn't going to get a knife to the chest or kidney fighting every day to keep from being extorted.

The last prisoner filed out and the guards left her there. As she was about to stand, Lieutenant Gibbs walked up the steps, her shoes clacking as she ascended. The pair made eye contact and she reached for the lever to shut the door. Shanea watched her the whole way. Gibbs pulled the lever and then the door closed. Gibbs didn't say a word. She just walked to Shanea and then sat across from her.

"Convict," Gibbs said. "I'm going to lay the ground rules for you."

Shanea nodded.

"First, you are my whore until I retire. Gonna be a long time before you see daylight," Gibbs said.

Shanea lunged at her. No better time than the present to go to isolation. Gibbs was ready and leaned to the side and snatched her in a choke hold before yanking her to her chest. "Fight it and I will hurt you," Gibbs barked in her ear as she tightened her grip, yanking Shanea off her seat with little effort.

Shanea gurgled and gasped as she fought to free herself, kicking out, clawing at Gibbs' hold. "Stop," Shanea gurgled. "Pleaaase."

Gibbs laughed and tightened her grip even more. "Stop… fighting," she growled.

Shanea stopped fighting as she started to black out. Her arms went limp and then Gibbs released her. Shanea fell into the center aisle with a loud cough and gasp of air. Gibbs yanked her up by the back of her collar and shoved her across the aisle to her seat. Shanea gasped and coughed, holding her throat as she did, chains clinking, face down, ass up. She heard Gibbs click her tongue. "Hmmm…hmmm, that motherfucker is *phat*."

Shanea immediately rolled over onto her back with a glare as she coughed one last time. The pair stared at one another, Shanea not bothering to hide the hatred coursing through her veins. Nothing was said as Shanea continued to rub her throat.

"Ready to listen?" Gibbs asked as if this were a regular occurrence.

Shanea slowly nodded.

"As I was saying, you will be my bitch. The warden wants to meet you and he has something in store for you too."

"Fuck you," Shanea growled. "I ain't no dyke."

Gibbs chuckled and then moved faster than Shanea expected her to. She snatched her by the front of her orange prison suit and held her nose to nose, Gibbs breath hot on her face. "So, you want to skip right to it, huh?"

Shanea tried to shake her off, but she couldn't. Truth was Shanea was a submissive at heart and the alpha female in front of her turned her on, and she had slept with her share of females in the neighborhood she grew up in.

Gibbs stared into her soft brown eyes. "Yeah, that's what I thought. Pussy getting wet?"

"No," Shanea snapped. "I'm strictly dickly," she growled. "I don't fuck bitches or fucking pigs. And you are *both*."

Gibbs laughed and didn't let her go, then she jabbed her in the side with her free hand doubling Shanea over. "I'm going to take you to private processing to check for contraband."

Shanea tried to jerk her face away, but Gibbs' grip was iron-tight. "Nod if you understand me."

Shanea gave a sharp nod and tried to turn away. Gibbs released her and then stood up and looked down at her. "On your feet, convict."

Gibbs stepped back and Shanea stood up. Gibbs towered over by six inches, and after a few quiet moments, Gibbs rotated to the side and Shanea went to move past her. Gibbs ran a palm across Shanea's lower back, then down to her ass cheek, and squeezed, causing Shanea to wince.

"I'ma bet that is gonna look good shaking in front of me," Gibbs hissed.

Shanea rolled her eyes at the comment and waited next to the lever. Gibbs reached around her and brushed Shanea's cheek with her own which made Shanea's clit throb with excitement. The door opened and Shanea turned and started down the stairs, her hands chained in front of her. When she reached the gravel-covered ground, she looked around. No one was in sight, only a bright strobe light that made her raise her hands to her brow to block it.

Gibbs stood behind her and said, "Walk to the yellow door across from you."

"I can't see it," Shanea grumbled.

"Walk in a straight line," Gibbs said. "Even a dumb rapper like you can do that, right?"

Shanea muttered under her breath and started to walk across the gravel, the stone crunching under her as she did. The yellow door was faded with a large plexiglass window in the center. As they approached, a guard's face appeared and then the door opened, and Shanea walked through. She gagged immediately. The room smelled like Lysol and bleach, over-whelming her senses.

Shanea stopped, unsure of where she should go. There was an open cage in front of her with a white male guard. On the ground, a foot away was a bright yellow line on an otherwise perfectly mopped white linoleum floor. Gibbs pressed her billy club in Shanea's lower back.

"Approach the line," she hissed.

Shanea walked forward and then stood at the line, her chains clinking as she walked. Gibbs walked beside her and then up to the cage. It was the first time Shanea had seen her back. Gibbs had a tight ass, more bubble than jiggle, and thighs that caught her eye. They touched which Shanea always found sexy.

Gibbs handed the guard a manilla folder she was carrying. "Prisoner Rollins, number 76134."

The guard in the cage took the envelope and stared at Shanea as he opened it. He pulled the paperwork from within and scanned it. He smirked, and then his eyebrows raised. "Judge gave ya the long haul, huh, hotshot?"

Shanea didn't respond as she checked out the room. White walls, white floor, and a bright yellow line, and that was it. The guard turned around and searched the table for a black and white uniform her size. He found it and brought it back to the counter.

"You got the search, LT?" he asked.

Gibbs took the paperwork with a nod before turning to look over her shoulder. "Prisoner Rollins, take the outfit and proceed to the door on your left and wait."

Shanea shuffled forward and took the black and white uniform in her hands barely able to hold it. She turned around and walked to the door and stood in front of it. Gibbs walked up behind her and slid an arm past her waist, lightly brushing it before popping open the lock. The door creaked as it opened, and Gibbs placed her palm on Shanea's back and pushed her in.

"Move, convict," Gibbs growled.

Shanea stood in the bare room with a single table and chair in the center. "Place your uniform on the table," Gibbs said as she went to close the door.

Shanea did as she was told and walked over to the table. She could feel Gibbs' eyes on her ass the whole way. Gibbs shut the door as Shanea stood with her back to her, the restraints swaying and clinking together as she waited. Shanea's heart thumped in her chest as she tried to control her breathing. She could hear Gibbs approach and closed her eyes.

Gibbs stood behind her and Shanea could feel her breath and her legs pressed against the back of hers. "Prisoner…" Gibbs growled.

"Yes?" Shanea managed to whisper.

"You will undress and ready yourself for a strip search," Gibbs said, stepping back.

Shanea gulped the lump in her throat and cleared it. Her fingers shook as she brought them up to her top buttons. She popped each silver button on her orange jumpsuit, her wrist restraints making it almost impossible to get it down. Shanea cut her eyes over at the chair. Gibbs pulled it across the floor, the screeching almost unbearable as she continued to unbutton her top.

She unbuttoned all of them and then raised her hands and shook her chains. "Now, how am I supposed to get this off?"

Gibbs chuckled behind her. Shanea felt her palm on her shoulder as she was turned around. "I guess I got to help you out of it, huh?" Gibbs said.

Shanea shook her cuffs again. "You could undo these and let me do it," she hissed.

Gibbs laughed. "Nah, I like controlling you."

Shanea couldn't help but be turned on by the statement. Why was she so horny? Why were these sadistic guards not in a prisoner's uniform with her? Surely, someone knew about it. Gibbs stared at Shanea's open jumpsuit. She reached her fingers up on each side and peeled them back, exposing her white undershirt. Gibbs licked her lips as she peeled the jumpsuit off her shoulders and left it at the crook of her elbows, locking her in.

"Gotta get this shirt off," Gibbs said, licking her lips.

Shanea rolled her eyes. "You can't just search me like this?"

"Nope," Gibbs said with a shrug, staring at Shanea's breasts. "I have to see what's under the bra."

Shanea tapped her foot and leaned away as Gibbs reached her hands in her jumpsuit and started to roll her shirt up her stomach and over her bra, exposing Shanea's breasts. Gibbs licked her lips again and then she lifted them and slid her hands around the bottom of her breasts. Shanea couldn't help but moan so quietly that it wasn't noticeable. She knew not to struggle, that could have serious consequences. Every few seconds the pair would make eye contact and Gibbs would smirk.

"Seems the fight has left you already, huh?" Gibbs said.

Shanea didn't say a word.

"I have to search you for *further* contraband," Gibbs said. "Assume the position."

Shanea glared at her. "How am I supposed to do that with my jumpsuit at my elbows and my hands cuffed?"

"You need help putting your hands on the table?" Gibbs asked.

Shanea frowned. "No."

Gibbs lifted her hand and twirled her index finger. Shanea grumbled under her breath and then turned back to the table and placed both palms on it. Gibbs kicked her feet apart and started her search.

She moved up her left leg, just below her privates, then her right. Shanea jumped when she felt both of Gibbs' hands go along her waistline and then over both ass cheeks and squeeze. Shanea cleared her throat and then she jumped again when she felt Gibbs' palm slide between her legs and rub it back and forth.

"Hmmmm…hmmm," Gibbs said when she felt the damp fabric. "Thought so."

"Whatever," Shanea snapped. "Just get the hell on with it. I'm not hiding anything, and definitely wouldn't stick anything up my cooch. Ain't no cell phone in there."

Gibbs chuckled and continued. Shanea knew what was going to happen next. "Ya know," Gibbs said. "I like tits."

"Who cares," Shanea mumbled as she cringed.

Gibbs leaned up against her back and started to squeeze them. "The underwire gonna have to go. It's *contra…band*."

Shanea rolled her eyes. "Really?"

Gibbs spun her back around, snatched her bra at the center, and ripped it in half, causing Shanea to gasp at the move as her breasts fell free. Shanea tried to cover up, but her cuffs wouldn't allow her to.

Gibbs slid a hand into her pocket and pulled her key out with an arrogant smirk at the power she had. "Guess I should unlock those now, huh?"

Shanea sucked her teeth. "You coulda done that a while back."

"Where's the fun in that?" Gibbs asked as she held the key up.

Shanea held her hands out as Gibbs stared at her breasts. Shanea cleared her throat. "You gonna unlock these or stare at my tits?"

Gibbs shrugged and then slid the key into the cuffs. "Yeah, it's getting late, and I've had enough fun for one evening."

When the lock clicked open, Shanea stepped back, her ass hitting the table, and rubbed her bruised wrists as Gibbs placed the chains on the table. Shanea tugged her orange jumpsuit over her breasts and waited. "Can I get some privacy to change?"

"Nope," Gibbs said, taking a seat nearby.

Shanea muttered under her breath and then turned around and started to strip out of her jumpsuit. She yanked the white shirt off and then held her arm across her breasts. She tugged the black and white prison shirt over to her and yanked it over her head as she did. She exhaled a loud breath and stopped.

"Something wrong?" Gibbs asked with a chuckle.

"You know I don't want to lower these coveralls with you staring at my ass."

Gibbs clicked her tongue and said, "If you want to get to your cell tonight, you better take them off."

Shanea exhaled a loud frustrated breath and then slid her hands to her waist and started to tug the fabric over her ass as quickly as possible, shimmying it over her wide hips. She heard Gibbs' quiet moan when the coveralls went over her ass cheeks, showcasing her black thong, and then down her thighs. Shanea kicked them aside and yanked her prison pants over.

"Panties too," Gibbs said.

"Fucking kidding me, right?" Shanea hissed. "You want me to go commando?"

Gibbs gave a nod to the clothes. "Pair in there."

Shanea unfolded the granny panties and picked them up. "Fuck," she hissed. "These things are hideous."

Shanea lifted a leg as Gibbs cocked her head to the side to see her pussy lips. She licked her lips as Shanea yanked the white panties on and then pulled the pants on right after it. Gibbs eyed her up and down with a smile. "Now, you look like a convict."

"Well, that was degrading," Shanea snapped. "And don't fucking remind me."

Gibbs stood up and shrugged. "Had to search you."

Shanea glared at her. "Not like that, you didn't."

Gibbs chuckled as she picked the cuffs and Shanea's panties up, shoving them in her pocket which made Shanea cringe. "My prison, my rules."

Gibbs stood behind Shanea and said, "Now, move through that door, convict."

Shanea started to walk through the room, leaving her orange jumpsuit behind. As she stood at the locked door and waited, Gibbs picked up a black phone on the wall. "Open three."

The door clicked and started to slide open. The noise from

the pod was deafening. The inmates pounded on the plexiglass as she stepped through, Gibbs right behind her. It seemed the entire pod was on the tier waiting for the biggest rapper in the world to walk into *their* world.

A young white CO with a baby face who could have shaved with a Kleenex started to approach them. "I got somethin' for ya, bitch," one of the inmates with five nappy cornrows shouted as she pounded on the glass beside her. Shanea swung her box braids over her shoulder and glared at the woman who flashed a razor blade in her mouth.

Shanea knew it would only be a matter of time. The young guard approached and said, "So, this is——-"

When he got within a foot of Shanea, she head-butted him and swept his legs out from under him. Gibbs snatched her baton and started to rain blows down on her, knocking her to the ground as more guards ran to help. Shanea collapsed onto the floor and curled up in a fetal position.

"Take her to the hole," Gibbs roared as she knelt beside the young guard.

Three guards yanked a groaning Shanea off the floor and dragged her down the hallway, feet loose behind her as the prisoners behind the plexiglass roared their approval, slamming their palms on the glass as they did. She wouldn't be getting any preferential treatment. When they reached the last door on the left, one guard unlocked it and the other two held her up as she swayed from the pain.

"Throw her ass in," one of the guards barked.

The other two guards readied to launch her into the hole and Shanea felt one of their grips loosen at the last moment so she wouldn't hit the wall as hard. Shanea stumbled forward when they threw her in and she hit the wall on the far side, banging her head as she did. She fell onto the floor with a shout of pain and curled up as several tears fell from her eyes.

"Brutus," Shanea heard a guard shout. "Seal it up."

"Yes, sir," Brutus said, sliding his hands to his keys and fiddling with them as he searched for the master key.

Shanea blinked the tears away, lifted her head and saw Brutus standing in the doorway looking down at her. He was a light-skinned giant close to seven feet with a massive chest and flat stomach that pretty much blocked out the door frame and hallway behind him. He was older with silver hair and long sideburns like the ones from the seventies. If Shanea had to guess, he was probably closing in on retirement. He glanced down the hall and waited a few moments and then instead of sealing it up, he slipped inside and closed the door until it was just a crack and hurried over to her.

"Hey, ya alright, kid," he asked in a deep rumbling voice.

Shanea winced and cleared her throat as Brutus helped her sit up against the wall. She gave a slight nod and patted her cornrows. "Yeah," she grumbled, then winced, feeling the bump forming.

Shanea made eye contact with him, his brown eyes soft and warm. Brutus smirked, then gave a light chuckle and said,

"You know that was the warden's nephew you just knocked out, right?"

"Oh, fucking great," Shanea sighed. "Just my luck."

Brutus put his palm on her shoulder, not in a sexual way but in a fatherly way. "Yeah, you're definitely gonna do some time in here. But I'm the head guard on this wing. Won't be no harassment from him." He clicked his tongue. "But if Gibbs comes down here, I can't do a thing."

Shanea nodded and asked, "I just knocked out one of your own. Why help me?"

Brutus shrugged and stood back up with a smile, dusting his hands off. "Cause he's a racist piece of shit. You did what I can't." He glanced over his shoulder. "I best be goin'."

"Okay," Shanea said.

Brutus turned and started to walk back to the door. "Hey, Brutus."

Brutus turned. "Yeah?"

"Been a while since I said it," Shanea said, pausing, causing Brutus to raise an eyebrow. "Thanks."

Brutus smiled again with a nod and then walked out and closed the door. Shanea heard the key enter the lock and then the bolt slammed shut, and with it her freedom. She winced as she slid up the wall, pushing herself up.

When Shanea made it to her feet, she surveyed the room. It was barren. Just a bed with a ratty paper-thin mattress, a sink, and a toilet that hadn't been cleaned in a long while, rust all over the chrome pieces. There was a small mirror above the sink and a bar of soap. She walked over to the bed and sat down, the frame groaning in protest. She placed her elbows on her knees, put her hands in her palms and started to cry.

It was the first time in a very long time that she did. And at twenty, with a sentence of twenty years, she knew that most of the years that counted were snuffed out. All that she had was hope. Hope for a new day, a new start. And a prayer that somehow she could score a phone to keep her raps up and send to the outside world. How she was going to record quality sound on the inside, she wasn't sure. But she was going to find a way…she always found a way.

The sentence she received should have gone to her boyfriend who escaped and went on the run. Who knows where he ended up? As she thought about Kayshawn or as the world knew him, Killa Two Times, a gangster rapper from College Park, her blood boiled. If she had just said no, she wouldn't be here. But true to the code, she didn't utter a word, even when they offered immunity. She would never break.

And the DA had everything she needed, even with all the money Shanea had, she couldn't beat the irrefutable evidence. They had her on camera with a close-up of her upper body when her plastic mask fell off as they broke into the vault, clubbing a security guard over the head with the butt of a gun as they did, hence the armed part of her robbery. The tattoo of Kayshawn's name on her neck was the dead giveaway and when the prosecution showed the evidence of it, she caught the whole charge.

As the sobs racked her body, her hands shook, and she clenched her fingers on her scalp which caused her to hiss in pain. The lump on top of her head was going to be large and painful. She yanked her fingers free and pulled her black and white striped forearm across her nose with a loud sniff. And with the palms of her hands, she smeared the tears away and sat in silence. All that went through her mind was the fact she needed to escape the shithole she now found herself in. And she would do anything in her power to achieve that and make for the border. Death was preferable to the twenty hanging over her head. If she could just get to the mil she buried in the forest by her home, she would be able to sneak out to a non-extradition country. It was time to hatch a plan.

Chapter 3

Shanea bolted upright when she heard the bolt on her door click open. She blinked and rubbed her eyes several times to clear the sleep as Gibbs stormed through the door with one of the bootlick trustees in tow. Shanea scampered back as they came in and she saw Brutus standing in the doorway with his arms folded across his chest watching Gibbs' every move, almost protective in a way.

"On your feet, convict," Gibbs barked, her eyes cold and menacing.

Shanea slowly rolled to the edge of the bed, feet dangling over the side, wincing when her body started to feel what the paper-thin mattress and the billy clubs had done to her after a few hours of rest. As she made it to her feet, the sun was starting to rise, sending tiny rays of light through her window.

Gibbs towered over Shanea and as she glared down at her, Shanea glared back up defiantly.

"On…your…feet," Gibbs growled, raising her club.

Shanea slowly rose to her feet with a long sigh, eyes focused on the club. She shook her arms out, rolled her neck, and then said, "Good morning?" she asked as a way of telling Gibbs she should have greeted her.

Gibbs smirked. "Oh, I'm gonna have a good morning." She paused and tapped her thigh with her baton. "You, not so much."

"And why's that?" Shanea asked as she stretched, drawing Gibbs, the trustee, and surprisingly Brutus' eyes who cleared his throat and looked away when she caught him with a slight smile catching her lips.

"Warden is sending you to gen pop," Gibbs said with a laugh, making Brutus raise an eyebrow. "You gonna get the treatment from the ladies courtesy of the house for smashing his nephew's head and putting him in the hospital."

"He's in the hospital?" Shanea asked, her heart thumping in her chest at the dreaded news. "He ain't…ain't dead, is he?"

Gibbs shook her head. "No, you gave him a concussion that will put him out of work for a week. Good thing your fuckery *didn't* kill him or you would be here for life instead of what the warden deems as a proper punishment added on for the assault."

"Fuck," Shanea grumbled, lowering her head with a shake. "My fucking luck to get more time."

Gibbs smiled and said, "It really shouldn't phase you."

"And why's that?" she grumbled.

Gibbs shrugged and stepped aside. "Cause you're prolly gonna have to knife a bitch in gen pop to get back to ad seg, giving you way more added time than assaulting one of my staff." She pointed at Brutus. "Now, follow Officer Miller."

Shanea raised her head and started to walk toward Brutus who stepped out into the hallway and held a pair of cuffs up. Shanea stopped and held her bruised wrists out. Brutus lowered them onto her flesh and instead of closing them tightly, he made it, so it looked like they were fastened, but loose enough to allow movement. Shanea looked at the cuffs and smiled.

Brutus stepped aside with a knowing nod and turned on his heel, walking down the linoleum hallway as the prisoners walked past them on the way to breakfast. Shanea kept her eyes straight ahead until she caught movement out of the corner of her eye.

Shanea gave a glance as the woman from the day before, minus her front two teeth lunged at her with a shank. Shanea spun and retreated, raising her hands to absorb the knife blow but the woman cried out just before it landed. Shanea backed into the concrete wall as Brutus yanked her attacker up by the wrist and pulled her arm out of its socket with a pop.

Shanea's face scrunched up when the woman gave a blood-curdling scream, the shank falling to the floor and making a loud clattering noise as the prisoner's cat called her attacker for getting caught before they were pushed forward by the guards in the back.

Brutus held her there as the other COs who were escorting the women to the chow hall rushed in and subdued her. Without a word, Brutus put his back to the woman and motioned for Shanea to walk by. Shanea started walking down the hall again and glanced over her shoulder as the woman was dragged away crying, clutching her shoulder. Shanea made eye contact with Brutus who nodded once more and walked behind her until they reached the end of the hallway, Gibbs and her crony a step behind.

Brutus gently moved her aside and slid a key into the lock and opened it, then stepped through. Shanea followed him and they continued down the next hall, Shanea's only accompaniment was the sound of the officer's shoes clacking on the linoleum. At the end of the hall was a set of double doors that Brutus opened and held open for her. Shanea walked in and stood in the center of the room for further instruction. Gibbs walked past her and bumped her shoulder.

Shanea growled as she staggered forward slightly. She watched Gibbs knock softly on the pane of frosted glass that had Warden Michael's stenciled on it. "Come in!"

Gibbs turned the brass handle to the door, removed her cap, and entered the office. She waved Shanea in, and she started to walk in with Brutus and Gibbs' trustee behind her. She glanced over her shoulder and caught Brutus staring at her ass. She turned back around before he could know he had been caught with a grin. Brutus would be her first mark on the climb out of the shitty rat hole she now found herself in. Whatever it takes to escape is whatever it takes, sex and all.

Shanea walked across the warden's Persian rug and waited in the center. The warden wasn't in his office. She tapped her foot as she looked around. On the back wall were bookcases filled with every trophy you can have for a nerd. Bowling, tennis, badminton. Typical white people's sports.

There were no books to speak of which didn't surprise Shanea at all. She heard the toilet flush on the far side of the room and the water run, then shut off. Shanea stared at the door as the warden emerged, wiping his hands on a towel.

And just as she expected, the warden was obese with what appeared to be small dick energy. He was balding with silver-streaked brown hair and a cul-de-sac on his head. His neck was flabby, and he walked with sort of a limp. To Shanea, he was disgusting. Anything to escape but *that*. He walked to his desk without saying anything and sat down. He ignored Shanea as he slid her dossier over to him, licked his finger, and flipped it open. Inside was her mugshot from jail after her arrest and the crimes she had committed. Linwood tapped his finger on his chin, jiggling his neck flesh and then looked up with a smile.

"So, twenty years it is," he said, tossing the file back on his desk with a smug look. "And now we get to decide how to deal with your fast-track idea to the box."

Shanea cleared her throat. "Look, I'm so—."

"Silence," Linwood barked. "I'll tell you when you can speak."

Shanea growled but didn't say anything. She didn't want to throw her chance for escape away, and depending on how the next few minutes went would decide how much additional time she would get, and what he would recommend for the DA to prosecute who already despised her.

Linwood looked at Gibbs and said, "You can leave, Lieutenant. And the cuffs won't be necessary."

"But, sir—"

A stern look from him stopped her cold, his eyes dead and void of any soul. Shanea snickered as Gibbs turned her head in Shanea's direction. "Something amusing, convict?" she barked, sliding her hand to the handle of her baton, Brutus' eyes moving to it as he grabbed his own.

"Nah," Shanea said, straightening her face and looking dead ahead at the warden.

"Lieutenant," Linwood said. "I'll call you when I'm ready for you to come back and get her." He flicked his finger. "Remove her cuffs."

Gibbs stared at Shanea for a moment longer, then yanked her hands forward, causing Shanea to wince. She slid the handcuff key in and removed the cuffs, sliding them onto her belt. Then she turned and walked to the door with the trustee and Brutus who opened the door for her. Brutus glanced at Shanea one more time and sighed before following Gibbs out and closing the door behind him.

When the trio left, the warden pointed to a plush seat in front of his desk. Shanea walked around the chair as the warden eyed her body up and down. The pair didn't speak as Shanea waited for him, adjusting her shirt several times to try and hide her breasts a little better without a bra having been given to her. She swung her box braids to the side so as not to lean against them in the chair as she rubbed her bruised wrists. It was uncomfortably silent in the room and all she could hear was the continuous tick of the clock to her right by the bathroom door.

The warden slid his hand to his phone and said, "Ya know, I found something interesting online."

Shanea raised an eyebrow in question but didn't say anything. The warden shrugged and held the phone up to his face and unlocked it. He scrolled for a minute, humming under his breath and then smiled. He turned the phone around and waved her forward. Shanea's heart sunk in her chest, and she lowered it. It was the dreaded leaked sex tape of her and two of her fans who she decided to sleep with to get back at Kayshawn when she caught him cheating with the ho-ass groupies after the concert in Atlanta a year prior. She had no idea there was a camera installed by one of her team that had extortion on his mind.

"Should I press play or should you?" he asked.

Shanea raised her head with a glare that bore through the warden, his shitty trophies, and his wall behind him. Linwood chuckled and then said, "I'll do it."

Shanea growled and her hands shook. If she lunged for him, she was done for. It wasn't like she hadn't seen it, and she felt bad for the two guys who were found out and both their wives left them and took their kids. Everyone lost in the scenario, although Shanea didn't blame her fans.

They didn't set the camera up. They just wanted to knock down the hottest rapper to come along after Nicki Minaj. It isn't every day you get to sleep with your favorite rapper. And when she heard Kayshawn lost his shit, it made it all worth the TMZ snitching tour. They were always ready to fuck someone over and had deep pockets to do it to turn a profit. Although her crew member who sold it to them was dead within a week. They found him face down in the street by his car with a twenty-dollar bill in his mouth and a note that said. *We sew bitches up in this hood.*

The rumor was that Kayshawn did it because it made him look like he couldn't keep his woman satisfied. And the cops didn't have anything to go on, so the case was dropped. Shortly thereafter, they robbed the bank, and she went to prison.

"Fuck…you, pig" she snarled.

Linwood smirked and then pressed play. "Exactly my thoughts, let's get to it then, shall we?"

Shanea watched herself getting double penetrated, the noises leaving her throat guttural, foreign, and harsh as her palms were planted on the ripped tattooed chest of the guy underneath her as she ground on his pelvis, her arch game perfect. She had seen it a dozen times and was numb to it now. She wasn't the first celeb, nor would she be the last. And she was proud of her body and how well she did fuck. Her arch made men cum within a few minutes. It could have been a whole lot more embarrassing.

Shanea's eyes leveled with Linwood's who turned the phone back to himself with a grin before shutting it off. "I've watched this a hundred times…" He slammed his palm on the table with a grin, causing Shanea's heart to thump. "And goddamn, you do some freaky ass shit, convict. I've never cum so hard watching a porno. That arch is perfection."

Shanea's whole body shook as she fought the urge to leap over the table and stomp his fat ass to death. It would be worth the life sentence. Hell, she was already doing twenty. What's another twenty added to it for that dirty prick jerking off to her?

But barely stopping her was the thought of her family, her nieces, and all the people who counted on her to one day come back home passed through her mind. If she could get that mil after an escape though, she could send money through some of her unknown associates to the feds to give to her parents. It was all she could do to calm herself and slowly slide back into the chair.

But she almost did leap again as she watched the warden slide his chair back a little and say, "I wanna find out how freaky you are myself with this cock in the back of your throat."

Chapter 4

"Ohhh, HELL NAH, YOU FUCKING PIG!" Shanea roared as she went to move to her feet.

Gibbs came barging in, baton high, and as she closed the distance, Linwood held his hand up. Gibbs stopped cold and lowered the baton. "Everything okay, Sir?"

Looking straight at Shanea, Linwood said, "I'm good, Lieutenant Gibbs. Our convict here was just voicing her disapproval of a proposition of not getting an additional *ten* years for assaulting one of ours and putting him in the hospital for my sister to call me every five minutes to give me a very much unneeded update with his stupid ass."

The ten-year comment made Shanea stop mid-way out of the chair. She seethed with anger as she took deep inhales and exhales of breath through her nose, her lips in a full-on sneer.

Gibbs didn't say anything, she just turned around and closed the door behind her on the way out.

"Got your attention now, *convict*?" Linwood asked with an evil grin. "You have no rights and no one in your corner. Your lawyer is finished with the case because you have no chance for appeal." He shrugged. "So, I have all the cards and you have nothing except the clothes on your back, and even I own those."

Shanea slowly lowered herself back into the chair, fuming. And Linwood was right…for the moment. He did hold all the cards and there wasn't anything she could do about it without a solid plan in place. She would make her escape and now it looked like she had to get him addicted to her kitty so she could put his ass to sleep and figure something out for the near future. If he got a taste, he would be bringing her to the office on the regular. And this is where her key to salvation was, that much she knew.

It wouldn't be the first time she used what God gave her to leverage a situation in her favor, not even close. She had been hustling since thirteen. The way she saw it, the other girls around her growing up gave it up after some weed and alcohol with the guys in the neighborhood, but she was cunning, very cunning. She would fuck the guys that owned recording studios in her neighborhood for free studio time to build her career as a condition for the kitty. And it had paid off very well. Made her a millionaire twice over in her short career.

Shanea looked around the office with an exaggerated sigh,

over her shoulder, and then glanced at the phone sitting in the middle of the desk and then back at him.

"What do you want?" she spat.

Linwood grinned ear to ear as he eyed her breasts while he licked his lips, then said, "I think you know the answer to that, convict."

Shanea rolled her eyes. "Yeah, kinda figured that's where we were going."

Linwood leaned forward, placed his forearms on the desk and then opened his hands wide. "Gibbs has told me that she told you how it was going to be on the tier where she controls the area. She loves her new fish wet and squirming right out of the shower as she likes to say. Me, on the other hand, holds the key to your freedom, wouldn't you say? And I like mine dirty and bent over a desk before breakfast."

Shanea scoffed, then sucked her teeth. "However, you look at it, *warden*, you'll be dead by the time I leave here. You can't help me especially if you gave me an extra ten."

Linwood laughed and leaned back in his chair, causing it to creak from his weight. "Maybe…maybe not. We shall see. I have more connections than you know in this state."

He flicked his index finger up a few times and Shanea raised an eyebrow. "Here?" she asked. "Now? You're fucking joking, right?"

Linwood smirked. "No, I'm not joking." He slid his chair back further. "It's my prison and I like a nice warm throat for my breakfast of champions to start my day."

Shanea balked at the statement. It wasn't even seven in the morning yet and this horny fat old white guy was trying to get some head before breakfast. Shanea waited a moment and collected herself, then stood up. Linwood slid his hand to his crotch and gave a nod to her breasts.

Shanea rolled her eyes and muttered, "Fine."

She slid her hands to the bottom of her striped shirt and rolled it over her flat stomach then lifted it over her head freeing her breasts. Linwood sucked in a gasp of air as he stared at her topless. Shanea tried to cover up, but Linwood snapped his fingers and she stopped then lowered her arms back down with a sigh, shirt by her side.

Linwood twirled his finger in the air and said, "Spin it."

"Spin it?" Shanea said. "For what?"

"So, you can yank those bottoms off and touch your toes so I can see that pink slit," he hissed.

Shanea balked, then turned and looked at the door. "Someone could come in."

Linwood laughed as Shanea distinctly heard his fly come down. "What and get fired?" He shook his head. "My staff knows what time it is. And they know not to interrupt. You're not the first, nor will you be the last."

"Ughhh," Shanea growled.

Linwood watched her spin slowly and stop. "The fuck you waitin' on, convict?" Linwood barked. "Touch your toes."

Shanea shook her head in disgust, her long box braids

swaying with her. She slid her hands to her hips and started to tug them down.

"Slower," Linwood gasped.

It was clear to Shanea that he had already started jerking his dick. She hoped that she had enough shake to make him cum so she wouldn't have to give him head but would that make him addicted to her kitty enough to slip in and steal his keys?

Shanea slowed her tease and then looked over her shoulder with a lower lip bite to give him a look that would make him jerk harder. When their eyes met, she knew she had him right where she wanted him, tongue loose, hand pumping under the desk.

"Should I stop, Sir?" she asked, knowing his kink already.

Linwood gasped and kept jerking, finally shaking his head. "No, convict," he gasped. "Keep, whew…" Linwood groaned. "Going."

Shanea slowly swayed her hips side to side as she bent over at the waist, tugging the black and white striped bottoms over her ass cheeks, their eyes locked. And for some reason, one she couldn't explain, her clit started to throb with need. It had been a solid six months of no dick and that felt like a lifetime. When she got halfway down her ass, she bunched the fabric in her fingers and tugged it down, then yanked both her cheeks up, popping them out as she stood back up.

"Fuck!" Linwood groaned as he blinked, his eyes glued to her ass.

Shanea snickered. Now who had the power?

With the slight tug of fabric over a perfectly round apple had him in the palm of her hand. It would be easier than she first anticipated. "Like this?" she asked, lowering the fabric and then yanking it back, making her cheeks jiggle.

"Goddamn!" Linwood gasped as he paused and raised his palm to his lips to spit in it before continuing. "Touch those toes."

Shanea rolled her eyes which he didn't even see as he stared at her. She slowly bent over at the waist again, rolling her pants off her thick thighs until they reached her ankles, then touched her toes, palms flat to the Persian rug.

"Oh my God," Linwood growled. "Now reach back and open your pussy."

Shanea huffed and then reached behind her and spread her lips, then gasped. She was soaking wet. Shanea glanced around her knee quickly and saw his jaw drop and watched him suck in deep breaths through his nose and exhale as his hand jerked faster and harder.

"Now," Linwood groaned. "Come finish this with your throat and knock those ten extra off the books."

Shanea stood back up with a suppressed groan of disgust and then kicked her pants to the side. She walked over to him, swaying her thick caramel hips which kept his eyes on her as she checked the room. She quickly searched his desk and didn't see his keys. Behind him on the table with his awards and pictures of his family…still nothing.

As she rounded the desk, Linwood spun in the chair. What she was expecting wasn't what met her eyes with his dick sticking straight. The warden was stacked with a dick that was at least nine if not close to ten inches but thin rather than thick. And without even thinking, she licked her lips. She preferred length to thickness. A really thick one hurt.

The pair made eye contact and Linwood slowed his hand. He slid his arms to the side and said, "Okay, convict. Showtime."

Shanea smirked and then slowly lowered to her knees and moved between Linwood's open legs, his dick twitching in anticipation as she did. His sack was ridged and firm with his balls as full as they were. Age hadn't caught up to his member like it had with the rest of his body.

Shanea readied herself and slid both hands up his thighs as she purred. "Do you want me to deepthroat it?" she asked as she reached the base.

Linwood only nodded as she slid her hands to his belt and undid it. The metal clinked as she pulled it aside, lifted it up and tugged his pants to his thighs. Shanea ran her fingers up to the edges and then started to tug them to his knees. As she did, his dick swayed side to side from the movement.

It was the first white dick she had ever seen and hopefully the last. She was only attracted to black men and that was as far as it went. But as a woman on a mission, she was ready to do whatever it took, even a shot to the mouth to get him relaxed enough to check his desk for the return stealth mission.

Shanea moved her head over the tip of his dick and slowly dripped some spit from between her pursed lips, eyes ever vigilant for the keys as she cut them at all the drawers behind his desk. She slid both hands to his pockets as she lowered down and took the tip in her mouth as she did to distract him, the hiss of approval enough for her to know it was working. And the keys weren't there. Shanea grumbled under her breath as she slid Linwood's dick into the back of her throat, gagging slightly as the tip reached her tonsils, and pushed past, her saliva starting to roll down along his shaft.

Shanea wedged her mouth side to side as Linwood groaned above her. There were three doors beside her on the desk. She slowly slid the tip to her cheek and tapped it as she glanced around him. "Ohhhh, you are a dirty girl, huh, convict?" Linwood groaned as he slid his hand onto the top of her head which caused Shanea to roll her eyes as she focused on the desk.

As far as she could see, she noticed three others behind the chair as she slid both hands to his shaft, jerking it while twisting them at the bottom of her lip. The top one was slightly ajar, and she nodded to herself. That would be the first place she looked as she switched positions and slid her palms to the chair, locking his legs in.

"Ughhh," Linwood groaned as he started to thrust.

The all too familiar *auuk* sounds started from her throat as she kept her mouth open and dug her nails into the fabric of the chair. Linwood stabbed her tonsils on each thrust. He slid his other palm onto her scalp and started to hammer. Shanea breathed in and out through her nose as he did, her spit slowly pooling at the base of his shaft. She felt his legs tense and knew he was ready.

With a shout, a hip shimmy, and a growl, Linwood came, and several small shots blasted from his tip. Shanea pushed forward with her knees, sliding his chair back as she slid her hands to his shaft, tightening her grip iron-tight, thumbs pressed together dead center to control him as her eyes locked in on the upper drawer that had a key sticking out of the lock.

"Woaaaaa," Linwood shouted. "Eassssssssssy!"

Shanea swallowed as he shot, pushing him further back until she was even with the drawer. Would he miss the key and know she took it? As Linwood came to a stop, his breathing labored, Shanea stopped and then released him. She moved back and watched Linwood undue his tie and hold his hand over his heart as he sucked in breaths, eyes clamped shut. Shanea cut her eyes quickly to the desk and just on top it were several paper clips in a pile.

She hurried to her feet and then leaned over and said, "Can you at least suck one of my nipples, Sir?"

Linwood groaned. "After that throat? Whew," he hissed before smacking her ass and turning her back toward the door, settling her ass cheek on his desk, her left hand not even an inch from the paperclips.

Linwood snatched both breasts roughly, causing her to wince as her fingers searched madly for the clips, she would need to pick the lock. She moaned in an attempt to keep him focused, although his biting them was starting to hurt. Her shaky fingertips pulled two of the clips to her and she brought one hand to the back of his head and leaned forward, pressing him to the back of his chair as he sucked.

"Hmmmmmmm," she moaned. "Yesssss. Fuck!" she hissed as she slid the paper clips between her ass cheeks and clenched them closed as she readied herself.

"I'm, gonna, cummmm," she moaned, placing both hands behind his head, pulling him closer, barely able to suppress the laugh as she faked her orgasm.

She shook her body for the full effect with a lip bite that almost drew blood to keep the laughter inside, and finally, Linwood pulled back with a gasp of air as she stood up, ass cheeks clenched.

"Whew," Linwood moaned as he blinked and then wiped his shirt across his sweat-drenched brow before rubbing it on his pants. "That was good."

"We square, warden?" Shanea asked, slowly backing away as she rubbed her clit to keep his eyes on her.

Linwood laughed and leaned back in the chair exhausted as he tugged his pants up. "For now, we are."

Shanea gave a fake smile and then walked to her pants and turned her back to the door as she slid them on, careful not to jostle the paper clips. She snatched her shirt and tugged it over her breasts as Linwood shouted, "Gibbs!"

Gibbs stormed in and looked at the warden as Shanea adjusted her clothes, feeling the paper clips in between her ass cheeks. They weren't going anywhere. Gibbs knew what had happened because she had next. She walked over to Shanea and slapped the cuffs on her with a frown.

"Take her to ad-seg for a bit longer," Linwood said as he cleared his throat. "I don't want her stabbed up…yet."

"Sah," Gibbs whispered, shoving Shanea by the shoulder toward the door. "Time for the showers, then *that* hole."

Shanea rolled her eyes at the comment and kept walking. Shanea walked up to Brutus who shook his head, causing Shanea to clear her throat and look away in shame. He knew what time it was too, and Shanea didn't even want to know how many women had been paraded through the warden on a power trip. All the other guards knew what time it was, and if you wanted to stay employed, you kept your mouth shut about it. He opened the door for her, and Shanea started to walk back down the hallway.

"Officer Miller," Gibbs said.

"Ma'am?"

"Attend the wing and dish out breakfast."

Brutus nodded and turned left at the intersecting halls. Shanea kept moving along without even looking at him, her stomach growling. She didn't want to give Gibbs any idea that she thought Brutus was attractive or a mark. Shanea continued to walk, not caring to have any conversation with her. As she walked, Shanea looked for an escape route for the future, and seeing none, she continued. It would take more than the warden's keys to escape. It wasn't as if she could slide out the front gate in a prison uniform. It was her first viable option.

As she walked past the next door, she saw the laundry machines and women working. Most of the laundry was prison uniforms at first glance but just as she passed by, she saw a few guard uniforms as well. She kept walking straight with an ear-to-ear grin. The next part of the plan would be in action soon.

When they reached the cell dorm it was the first time Gibbs turned her back on Shanea. Shanea got a glance at her apple ass and then the thought ran through her mind to jump Gibbs and take whatever consequences there were to come. But as she took a step forward, Gibbs glanced over her shoulder as she unbolted the door. "You really want to do that? Cause I won't stop beating you until I hear something crack."

Gibbs opened the door with a smirk and turned to the side to let Shanea pass.

As she did, Gibbs raised her baton and tapped Shanea on the ass, and said, "I got something for that ass tonight."

The door creaked open, and Shanea walked through. She looked at her bed and on it was a change of underwear, a prison-approved bra and a black teddy. Toothpaste, a toothbrush and oil for her hair. Shanea swung her head around and looked at Gibbs who cracked a smile.

"I not as mean as you think I am," Gibbs said with a shrug. "You needed to know who the boss is."

Shanea nodded.

"So, I'll be back tonight when I run the wing on my double and you'll have that black teddy on and ready to eat my pussy. I've taken the liberty to have the cameras shut off for tonight's festivities. I'll be taking the teddy with me when I leave."

Shanea growled at what Gibbs was going to make her do but nodded, nonetheless. Gibbs walked out and closed the door behind her, the deadbolt locking a moment later. Shanea waited for a moment as she studied her room, looking for the perfect place to hide them. As she walked along the wall that the bed was against, she noticed that the grout under the sink had broken off in parts. She knelt under it and inspected the area. Just below the sink where the pipe went through with no clearance, Shanea saw a spot where she could slide the paperclips in where the grout had rotted away.

Shanea glanced over her shoulder, then reached in the back of her pants and pulled the paperclips out. She slid them into the open area and then stood back up. It was unlikely any of the guards had even noticed. But to make sure, Shanea slid her sandal under and swiped the granules of concrete from the area. She walked to her bed and picked up her toothpaste and toothbrush. Shanea walked to the sink and started to brush her teeth. It was the first time she had looked in the mirror and the lump on her head was sticking up slightly. Shanea winced when she felt it and then spat the toothpaste into the sink.

She placed them on the back ledge and walked over to her bed. The lacy black teddy stared her straight in the face. Beside it was a stick of a no-name deodorant and she leaned into her armpits and sniffed, wrinkling her nose. She picked it up and then lifted her shirt, rolling it under her arms as she did with a sigh of relief. There was a single Bic razor blade and a small amount of shaving cream. Shanea longed for a shower and that wasn't going to be anytime soon. It was time for a clean-up and to wait until nightfall for Gibbs to return.

Shanea slept most of the day, only getting up when Brutus brought her breakfast and lunch, which at best was disgusting. And just before the dinner chow, she heard the bolt on her door unlock. Shanea moved a little under the covers to make sure that if it was Brutus, he wouldn't see her in the nighty. The door creaked open and in front of her stood Gibbs. The pair locked eyes and Shanea noticed that Gibbs' grey shirt had the first three buttons undone.

"Convict," Gibbs said in greeting, walking in and closing the door behind her.

"Hey," Shanea said as she pulled her covers closer.

"You ready for me to cum all over your pretty face?" Gibbs asked approaching, pulling her baton from its sheath on her side.

Shanea stared at the baton that had already hit her several times and scooted back. "I'm not gonna hit ya," Gibbs said as she moved it to the top of the blanket and slowly tugged it down. "Not with this anyway."

Shanea fought it for a moment but stopped when she realized the faster she got this over with, the better off she would be, and the closer to escape. As the blanket lowered, Shanea watched Gibbs lick her lips. In all honesty, Shanea was getting wet under the blanket and the black lace was rubbing her skin just right for her to want to masturbate under the covers.

The blanket lowered halfway down her pressed-up caramel breasts and Gibbs moaned, "Bet those long nipples need to be sucked on, huh?"

Shanea cleared her throat in response, afraid it might crack. Was it that obvious that her nipples needed a pair of full lips on them? And Gibbs definitely had those. "You can nod, con…" Gibbs slid the end of her baton to Shanea's right nipple and rubbed it in circles, eliciting a long moan from Shanea, "vict. I know you need some good head."

Shanea slowly nodded as her skin flushed. Yes, she did feel sexy, and yes, she wanted her nipples sucked on and some good head which she hadn't had in months either. Gibbs slid the baton down between her breasts which Shanea watched. Gibbs lowered it to the point where the baton made it to the bottom and then drew it back up her skin, sliding it under the strap on her right shoulder.

Shanea looked away and bit her bottom lip, gnawing on it

as Gibbs slid it under the left strap and then down her arm, goose-bumping her flesh. Shanea felt the baton lift her chin and the pair made eye contact as Gibbs used her free hand to unbutton her grey shirt the rest of the way.

"Still strictly dickly?" Gibbs asked as she pulled the baton away from Shanea's chin and slid it back into her holster. "Cause I *know* that was a fucking lie yesterday."

Shanea cleared her throat as her juices leaked onto her bed. She shook her head slowly and sighed with a shrug. "Nah, I eat pussy too."

Gibbs slid a finger to Shanea's cheek, towering above her, and said, "Even if you didn't, you were gonna tonight, ain't that right?"

Shanea swallowed the lump in her throat and nodded at the alpha energy. It took everything not to slide a hand to her clit and rub the throbbing away. Or not pinch one of her nipples and tug it slowly, twisting it just slightly.

"That's right," Gibbs said with a chuckle, sliding her hand back and tugging her shirt from her tight pants. "Now, take the blanket off and stand up."

Shanea slowly slid the blanket the rest of the way off and then scooted to the edge of the bed; the black teddy straps pooled at her elbows. Gibbs tugged her shirt off and placed it on the sink nearby. Shanea stared at her upper body which was muscular and solid. Her breasts were small, a palm full at best. But that turned Shanea on as she only liked small breasts and very large asses.

Shanea stood on shaky legs and tried to tug the short nighty down over her ass cheeks, but it stayed right where it fell at halfway, just a little too tight to be comfortable but that wasn't Gibbs' plan anyway. Shanea was just thankful it fit somewhat and didn't leave all of her hanging out. Her skin prickled from the freezing air, her nipples hard as pebbles, pressing the black fabric out.

Gibbs gave a sharp head nod with a stern look at Shanea's breasts. She got the message and slowly started to roll the top down. Her caramel breasts fell free and she looked away. "That's what I'm talking bout, girl," Gibbs moaned.

Gibbs slid her hands behind her back, undid her white bra and pulled it off. Shanea stared at her long nipples, slight stretch marks on the side of each breast. Gibbs finger waved her forward and then pointed to her left one.

"Suck it, convict," she growled.

Shanea stepped forward and leaned over at the waist, taking it in between her lips. Gibbs smelled so good with her Chanel on. Shanea started to suck and kept her hands by her side. Gibbs reached down and yanked Shanea's hand to her large ass cheek and placed it there.

Shanea sucked, massaging Gibbs' ass cheek and with the other, she grabbed her other breast and kneaded the flesh. Gibbs let out a long moan as she crept her hand along Shanea's side and then violently smacked her ass, making Shanea rear back.

"Ouch! That fucking hurt," Shanea shouted, rubbing the sting away.

"Oh?" Gibbs hissed before spinning Shanea around, who yelped and shoved her toward the bed. "You ain't seen shit yet, convict."

Shanea stumbled to the bed, the back of her nighty riding up to her lower back as she caught herself with both palms on the bed frame, her pussy starting to soak. She had to bite her lip to block the moan escaping her lips. Gibbs walked up behind her, leaned over her back, and snatched her by the back of the neck, causing Shanea to cry out.

"Shake…it," she growled. "Understand?"

Shanea hurried to nod but gasped when she felt Gibbs kick her legs open and slide her palm underneath her and then directly across her soaked slit. It felt so good, she didn't want to move.

"I'm waiting," Gibbs snarled.

Shanea moaned as Gibbs rubbed her fingers in her folds, curling them toward her clit as she slid her free hand to snatch her braids, arching her neck. Shanea arched her back, rolling her neck back further, chin jutting out in front of her, and started to grind across Gibbs' palm with a groan of pleasure.

Whether or not she was being forced, Shanea was starting to get into it as the moans started escaping her lips. "Uh, huh…" Gibbs groaned as she pulled her palm away and swung it around Shanea's face, holding it right to her lips. "You soaking my fingers. Suck them clean."

Gibbs leaned further forward and straightened all four fingers that were slick with Shanea's juices, and Shanea eagerly deep-throated them with a loud gag, making her clit buzz as Gibbs' fingernails tickled her tonsils as she released her braids, lowering her head and removing her fingers.

"Good girl," Gibbs said, sliding her cleaned hand away and standing to the side.

Shanea spun her head with a smile and stared into Gibbs' eyes and then started to twerk, her caramel cheeks colliding with loud smacks of skin in the silent room, the sound reverberating off the walls as she did. Gibbs' eyes stayed glued to them as she watched Shanea's skin jiggle. Shanea knew she had her where she wanted her…ready to fuck.

Shanea watched Gibbs raise a hand in the air, their eyes locked. Shanea bit her lip and watched her bring it down on her ass cheek, yelping each time it struck her as she continued to twerk. The cracks to her skin made her cry out. Gibbs gave a low chuckle and then did it again, and again and again until Shanea's right cheek was pure red.

Gibbs slid her hand to Shanea's pussy lips again and then slowly slid all four fingers in her. Shanea expelled a loud whoosh of air as her eyes rolled and a deep guttural groan escaped her throat. It had been the first time she had been penetrated in months and it felt so good.

"Yeah," Gibbs moaned as she started to corkscrew her fingers into her sloshing juices. "You like it rough."

Shanea came without warning, thinking about a strong

black man behind her, fucking her as hard and as fast as he could. Her whole body seized up at the thought as her upper lip curled and her eyes crossed.

"Fuck!" Shanea screeched as she angled her pelvis against Gibbs' fingers, riding it as if it were a dick.

Gibbs licked her lips and watched as Shanea fucked her hand, her ass cheeks colliding and almost driving Gibbs to a knee as Shanea fucked her. It only lasted a moment before Gibbs got the upper hand and muscled Shanea onto her stomach and laid over her as she continued to rub Shanea's G-spot until she started to whimper, and her body jerked every few seconds before she held her hand up. Gibbs smirked and then slowly withdrew her drenched fingers and then smeared the juices on Shanea's red ass as she took deep breaths to control her heart rate.

"Fuck," Shanea groaned as she curled up into a fetal position. "That was intense."

"You ain't seen shit yet, convict," Gibbs said, stepping back and yanking her baton free.

She unhooked her belt and lowered it to the floor. Gibbs unbuttoned her pants and then pulled them over her ass cheeks as she turned around and pulled them up with the fabric, making Shanea's clit twitch.

Gibbs tapped her ass cheek with her palm and said, "You ain't the only one with a phat ass in here."

Shanea giggled and then watched Gibbs bend over and pull them the rest of the way off, her white thong drawing

Shanea's eyes to her dark skin. It was time to make Gibbs addicted to her kitty and get another step closer. Shanea sprung to her feet and hurried to Gibbs who was bent completely over at the waist, pooling her pants to pick them up.

Shanea peeled Gibbs' ass cheeks apart and slid her long tongue between her outer lips, starting to move it around as fast as she could, tasting her juices which made her moan. Gibbs gasped and then gave a long moan herself as she grabbed her calves for Shanea to dig in.

"You nasty ass, bi——." Gibbs' hips wiggled, then she opened one of her cheeks wider and gasped, "Faster, bitch! Immma.... Immma cummmmmmmm!"

Shanea slid a hand around Gibbs's waist and started to rub her clit in circles as she did. The sound of the slurping turned Shanea on as she continued, sliding her free hand to her clit to rub it, Gibbs' large dark ass cheeks now smothering her face.

"Shit!" Gibbs shouted as Shanea felt her juices start to soak her chin. "Immma nuttttt!"

Gibbs threw both palms on her knees and arched her back, lifting slightly for Shanea to wiggle her tongue side to side as she swallowed the juices sliding onto her tongue. "Fuccccck!" Gibbs cried out as her body shook and she pounded both her palms rapidly on her kneecaps.

As Gibbs' orgasm passed, Shanea leaned back and took a loud gulp of air and then exhaled and waited for what Gibbs would do next. Shanea slid her hand from Gibbs' clit and knelt just behind her as Gibbs took deep breaths. "Fuck, convict," Gibbs gasped as she fanned herself. "You shoulda been a porn-star with that tongue."

Shanea laughed for the first time in a long time. She shook her head with a smile and waited for Gibbs who slowly slid a hand to her baton which made Shanea slide back. Gibbs laughed and stood up, her perfect chocolate ass just inches from Shanea's lips. She turned around, baton tight in her hand, Shanea's view switching to her slit.

"Look up, convict," Gibbs growled.

Shanea slowly moved her gaze up Gibbs' flat stomach, over to the baton and then up to her face. Gibbs had a grin on her face and then said, "Face the wall on your knees on the bed, convict."

Shanea looked over her shoulder then up at Gibbs who twirled her finger and mouthed, "Up…convict."

Shanea sighed. There was no telling what was about to happen. Before she made it to her feet, Shanea saw Gibbs' keys lying nearby. The carabiner she had them hooked to was an easy one to yank off. If she could manage to get both Gibbs and the warden in the same room, snag both sets, she could try to figure out a way to incapacitate them. But coming up with something that could do that would take a lot of planning before she could make her move. Time she didn't have.

Shanea slid onto the bed and moved into doggy style. She placed her ear on the comforter looking at the door and twerked. She froze when she felt the cold wood of the baton slide up and down her slit. Shanea felt Gibbs slide over her ass cheek as she rubbed her slit with the baton.

"I left my strap on at home. This is gonna have to do," she moaned before flicking Shanea's earlobe, sending shivers up her spine.

"You're…you're not—"

"Bet your…" Gibbs slowly slid an inch in. "Sweet pussy I am."

Shanea's jaw dropped instantly. "Gawd," she groaned after a quiet moment as she looked over her shoulder at the baton being inserted into her slowly. "That feels so good."

"Arch your back," Gibbs moaned, tugging one of her nipples.

"Fuck!" Shanea moaned as she arched her back and turned to watch it disappear.

Shanea groaned and reached one hand to her ass cheek to hold it open, spreading it wide, causing Gibbs to lick her lips. Shanea gnawed her bottom lip as inch after inch sunk into her. She whimpered when ten inches, almost to the cross handle buried in her.

"Jesus," Shanea hissed as she started to slide forward and back, fucking the baton like a sex toy. "I can't believe I'm doing this."

Gibbs reached down and rubbed her clit as she fucked Shanea with it. Shanea threw it back on the slick veneer until a wave of pleasure started to flood through her. She came hard, clutching the sheet as her eyes rolled from the feeling. Shanea pitched forward, holding her slit tight as her body bucked up and down. Gibbs chuckled and pulled the baton away and pushed it in the sink to wash it. With Gibbs' back turned, Shanea eyed the keys and saw the long master key immediately. That would be hard to steal but she was going to make the move in one swoop, and if she could somehow manage to tie them up, it may work, or she would be sent to a dark dreary place beneath the prison for twenty years. But right then and there she decided the juice was worth the squeeze.

Chapter 6

Shanea woke the next morning when she heard a guard bark, "Breakfast!"

The slit in the door flicked open and Shanea bolted from the bed and took it. She winced as she walked back to the bed. Her pussy was sore after the baton. She made it to the bed and sat down in her prison-issued garb, having changed before Gibbs left with the teddy to destroy the evidence.

In truth, Shanea had never had such powerful orgasms in her life. She stared off into space as she ate her powered eggs with the plastic fork that had been issued with no knife. The sausage links were rock hard and still half frozen. Shanea sighed as she continued to grind the food in between her teeth. Twenty years of that wasn't going to happen.

Once she finished, Shanea rose to her feet and stretched

with a long yawn, then shook her head and walked to the mirror. She brushed her teeth and then splashed water on her face, which was lukewarm at its hottest temperature. She sniffed under her pits and shook her head with a frown. A shower couldn't come fast enough. As she washed her face, she heard the distinct tap of a baton on her metal door.

"Ms. Rollins," Brutus said in his deep grumbling voice. "I'm coming in."

Shanea fluffed her box braids and adjusted her top, looking in the mirror. The deadbolt on the door clicked and opened. Blocking the doorway with his massive frame was Brutus with his tight work shirt. "It is time for your shower before you report for work," he said.

"Okay," Shanea said, turning around and walking to the bed. "What's my job?"

"You will be in the laundry."

Shanea shook her head and puckered her lips, then frowned. That was going to be a hot job and with the steam she saw yesterday, it would be easy for another prisoner to shank her. But where there is a will, there is a way. That would be the best place to sneak out pieces of an officer's uniform. "Hey, Brutus," Shanea said, checking her teeth.

"Yeah?"

"I wanted to thank you for taking care of the heffa who was going to stab me yesterday," she said.

"Just doing my job," Brutus said, flicking some imaginary lint off his shirt sleeve.

"Well, thanks anyway. If there is anything I can ever do to repay you, just let me know."

Brutus gulped the lump in his throat as Shanea walked away from the sink. She cut her eyes in the mirror and watched Brutus' eyes follow her ass cheeks as they indented. Shanea grinned with a quick nod. Yup, he would be easy prey to seduce, and get him ready to assist in any way he could for her escape. He would just take a nudge in the right direction. Shanea took longer than she needed when she bent over to get her slippers under the bed. She heard Brutus clear his throat as she reached under the bed, turning her head slightly as she did, her braids dropping over her shoulder.

"You should see it in a thong," Shanea said with a laugh. "These pants don't do it justice."

All Brutus did was clear his throat again and then grumble, "Let's go."

"Sure thing, Brutus," Shanea said, slipping into the green loafers and turning back around.

She snatched her scratchy folded white towel with a bar of soap and made her way over to him. Brutus stepped back and held the cuffs out. Shanea held her hands out, staring up at him innocently and Brutus applied them to her wrists. And just like last time, he didn't tighten them too tight. As Shanea was about to take a step, Brutus held his hand up reached behind his back, pulled out a pair of leg shackles, and dropped to one knee.

"Seriously?" Shanea spat.

Brutus shrugged as he clasped them around her ankles and then stood back up. "Warden's orders." He paused and cracked a slight smile. "You did assault one of the guards which now makes you high risk."

"Oh, c'mon, Brutus." She gave a head nod to the plexiglass where the other women were gathering to get a glimpse of the famous one. "You woulda done the same with those skanks waiting to kill or maim you for cred."

Brutus made sure no one saw him smile and said, "Yep… and I ain't shed a tear over that boy getting his head beat in. And the reason I'm not tightening these cuffs as a thank you for what I couldn't do."

His face went to stone, and he turned to the side and pointed down the hall. "After you, Ms. Rollins."

Shanea started to walk to the showers which she had passed on the way to the warden's the day before and proceeded past the inmates who started to pound on the plexiglass. The leg irons made it to where she needed to shuffle in place, the metal clinking on the floor as she did, her braids swaying on her back as she continued. Shanea kept her head held high and didn't glance at any of them.

"Yo, rich ho!" one of them shouted, making her roll her eyes.

"She fittin' to be my bitch!" shouted another before they cleared the window and down to the shower.

Shanea made it to the showers and entered. The showers were white laminate, and it appeared the shower heads didn't have any rust on them. It was empty as was required for high-risk prisoners in Belmont, with too many stabbings when everyone showered together. Shanea stopped and waited for Brutus who walked past her and knelt by her ankles, removing the cuffs before standing back up.

Shanea held her hands out, looking up into his eyes as he towered above her, and Brutus unlocked those as well, sliding them onto his belt. "Thanks, Brutus," Shanea said, rubbing her wrists as she walked in. "Where do I put my clothes?"

Brutus pointed to a hook near the closest shower head and Shanea started to walk to it. "I'll be right outside. You can have privacy when I'm around, Ms. Rollins. I don't think you'll try anything with me."

Shanea gave a smile and said, "Thank you, Brutus. I'm sure that will be far and few in between. And no, you're the only one who has been nice to me so I won't make it so you have to *hurt* me."

Brutus smiled with a raised eyebrow; the first reaction she had seen him make. Was it because she emphasized the word hurt. Was that his kink? Calm giant to everyone around him, but in a bedroom very domineering with "leave a mark" energy? Shanea felt her clit throb at the thought of a heavy-handed giant dominating her, ass up, face down buried in her pillow screaming murder. She was submissive in the bedroom as a release for being so alpha in the real world as someone from the streets. Gibbs had pegged that about her first thing out the gate.

Breaking up her thoughts of what he could do to her, Brutus said, "You have ten minutes…if you can stand it."

"Okay, I'm moving," Shanea said as she lifted her towel and placed it on the hook near the entrance to set a trap to catch a giant.

Brutus walked around the corner and waited as Shanea started to undress and place her clothes out of the range of the water. As she did, the thought of why he was so nice went through her head. She reached out to the faucet and turned it on and that was a mistake as the ice-cold water hit her naked body straight on.

She moved out of the way and shouted, "Fuck!"

"Everything alright, Ms. Rollins?" Brutus asked from the other side of the wall.

"Yeahhh," Shanea grumbled. "Fucking water is like an ice bath."

She heard Brutus' grumbling laugh on the other side of the wall. "I said if you could stand it. It will warm up in a minute."

Shanea snickered and said, "Oh, believe me, I can deal with a lot of pain, Brutus."

Brutus cleared his throat again. Oh yeah, she had his ass dead to rights. It had to do with his doling out of pain behind a closed door. Shanea held her breath and stepped into the freezing water and then immediately exhaled it sharply as it took her breath away. Her nipples instantly hardened, her skin goose bumped, and her teeth chattered after a moment.

She hurried with the soap, but her hands shook from the cold. She stepped back, just out of the range of the spray, and rubbed her arms up and down her biceps as she stood freezing. Then the water started to warm, and steam started to float up around her. She sighed and then stepped back in. And although it was lukewarm, it sure as hell beat the freezing temperature.

Shanea rubbed the soap all over her body for the next several minutes, thinking of Brutus. Did he have a huge dick or was his size average? She bit her bottom lip and gnawed on it when she thought of him lifting her above his head which he could easily do. She had only had that twice and both times she was down for the count afterward.

Shanea glanced at the towel as she spit the water out of her mouth, rubbing her upper body and underarms with the soap before washing clean. She turned sideways and looked to see if Brutus was leaning around the corner staring, but he wasn't.

Shanea smiled and then shut the water off. "Brutus," she called out.

"Yeah?" Brutus said, still nowhere within sight.

"I…uh, I forgot to bring my towel with me, and I'm afraid of slipping on the floor to get it. Could you help me?" Shanea asked in her most innocent voice even as her clit throbbed and made her almost touch it.

It was quiet for a long moment, and she saw Brutus' massive hand sneak around the corner, lift the towel off the hook and hold it a few inches further back, nowhere close to where it needed to be.

Shanea snickered and said, "Brutus, not even close."

She heard Brutus sigh and then click his mic on his uniform and say, "The prisoner needs her towel, Tim. Over."

"Why tell me, over," Shanea heard Tim chuckle as Brutus released his button.

"You're manning the cameras, dummy," Brutus growled. "I'm not trying to get fired my final few months here. Over."

Shanea bit her lip to stop from guffawing at Brutus attempting to help her. He was a nice guy as any other guard would have told her no and would have let her slip and smack her tailbone.

"Copy that," Shanea heard Tim squawk back. "Camera five is off."

"Copy," Brutus sighed. "Ms. Rollins, I can't turn my back to you."

"Annnnnd?" Shanea giggled.

Brutus gave a long sigh. "My wife would not have approved of me seeing you like that."

Shanea's heart sunk. Just her luck. As nice a guy as Brutus was, he wasn't the type to cheat. "Fuck," Shanea hissed.

Shanea thought on her feet as quickly as she could. Then it came to her. "Ummm…yeah, so, ummmm, would she want you to leave a woman freezing in the shower to catch a cold in this shithole."

It was quiet for a very long moment and then she heard Brutus sigh. "No…no she wouldn't have."

Shanea raised an eyebrow at the last statement. No, she wouldn't have. "You keep talking in past tense," Shanea said.

It was quiet for a long moment and then Brutus said, "She has passed."

"I'm sorry, Brutus," Shanea said.

"It's okay."

"Anyway, can you help a sista out?" she asked, making sure her teeth chattered harder than they needed, standing shoulder width apart and waiting for the trap to spring. "Before my tits fall off."

She heard Brutus snicker and then she watched his grey uniform shirt turn the corner. Brutus moved around the corner, his shiny black shoes clacking on the tile as he did. His head was to the side but after a step, he couldn't see the puddles and his foot slid a few inches.

"Shit," Brutus muttered before turning his head and checking the tile for puddles. "My old ass can't take a fall like that."

His eyes slowly moved up Shanea's shins, over her knees, stopping on her thick thighs that touched as she grinned when the trap sprang. He stared at her shaved mound, then up her flat stomach, and stopped on her breasts, nipples hard as rocks.

"Ah…hem," Shanea said, doing everything in her power not to laugh.

Game…set…match, and now it was on and poppin'.

Chapter 7

rutus blushed and cleared his throat as he looked away. Shanea waited for his soft brown eyes to filter back to her body as she stepped forward one step. She let her breasts sway to bring his attention back, which it did. Shanea gave a coy smile and made sure her fingers brushed the tops of his as she took the towel.

"Thank you," she said, pulling it back before letting it drop from her fingers onto the wet tile. She shrugged and said, "Oops."

Brutus blushed even more, swallowing the lump in his throat as he tugged his grey shirt collar to release some of the steam rising from his neck. As Shanea bent over to pick it up, she drew Brutus' eyes to her ass cheeks. She cocked her head to the side as Brutus tried to avert his eyes, but they returned immediately as the water dripped from her body. The bulge she saw made her jaw drop. It was the thickest shaft that she had ever seen, hugging the grey fabric to mid-thigh. Shanea gasped and then slid her shaky fingers to the towel and quickly stood back up. She slammed her thighs together and suppressed her moan for the moment. There was no reason to scare off her prey, she just needed to coach him through it. If a man is hard, you can always close that deal, always.

"Am I making you uncomfortable, Brutus?" Shanea asked, sliding the towel halfway up her breasts, barely covering her nipples.

"Yes," Brutus whispered with his eyes telling her he was at his weakest point.

Shanea pouted and stepped closer, running her palm up his bicep, making Brutus give a low moan. "I'm sorry." She paused and then said, "Should I put my uniform back on so you can take me back to my cell?"

Brutus didn't say anything for a long moment and then slowly nodded as his eyes settled on her breasts again. She had him on the ropes. One more little nudge. She cocked her head to the side again as he watched her and then she grinned at his hard-on.

She made eye contact with him. "So, you want me to go back to the cell, but *that…monster*." She shivered slightly at the thought of it buried to the hilt inside her. "Is telling me you want me to bend over and touch my toes so you can smack me really really hard."

Brutus cleared his throat as his member grew another inch and a bead of precum stained his pants, making Shanea gnaw her lip. "Yeah," Shanea said with a nodding grin. "It's the domination you like, huh?" She amped it up. "You need a little young thingy to slap around like the old days, huh? Been too long, hasn't it?"

Brutus couldn't stop himself. He nodded extremely slowly, almost deliberately as he suddenly licked his lips. "Do you want to see them again, Brutus?" Shanea cooed, stepping closer. "Maybe you can pinch 'em really hard till I whimper. I know that's what you want. Wanna know a secret?"

Brutus swallowed the lump in his throat. "Yes," he croaked.

"You wanna know how I like it from behind?" Shanea moaned.

"Yes," Brutus managed to croak out again.

Shanea bit her pinky nail and said, "Rough and hard, face down, ass up, putting me in place to…obey."

Brutus' eyes bored through her scratchy white towel, but he remained silent after the comment. Shanea reached over and slid her fingers into his, making hers disappear, and then lifted it to the front of her breasts.

"Sooooo, how much do you want a young chick like me bouncing on your fat dick in here?" she moaned a little louder, stepping closer so only a few inches separated them, his palm just barely touching the fabric as he towered above her.

"Cause I need a strong black man handling business. I know these skeeza's try, but they ain't got what I got, huh?"

Brutus slowly shook his head from side to side.

"You wanna…help?"

Brutus moved so fast that Shanea squealed as he lifted her over his shoulder like a sack of potatoes, her arms flying wide behind his back, fingertips grazing his keys as her box braids swung over her shoulders. He made his way to the very back showers out of view of everyone.

"That's what I'm talking bout!" Shanea shouted with raucous laughter.

Shanea winced when Brutus swung his massive free palm across his chest and smacked her ass cheek so viciously that she bit her lip.

"Quiet," he hissed.

"Okay, Daddy!" Shanea moaned as she rubbed her pussy across his shoulder as hard as she could to get some relief.

Shanea yelped when Brutus lifted her over his shoulder, her head just barely missing the ceiling, and then held her in a one-handed bear hug by the lower back, her breasts in front of his lips, bicep bulging as he held her. With his free hand, Brutus reached up and yanked the towel open, causing her to gasp and immediately swing her hands around the back of his neck as she shoved her nipple in his open mouth. It felt like a vice clamped down on it as Brutus inhaled it.

"Ohhh…myyyy…gaaaawd," Shanea groaned, leaning her ear over the top of his head with a loud groan of approval, listening to the sucking sounds as she massaged the back of his neck with a grin. "Just like that."

Shanea held onto him for what seemed like an hour as she had her eyes pinched shut to just enjoy the feeling and block out the fact that these shower heads would be a constant companion for the next twenty years if she couldn't escape. When the thought crossed her mind about the finality of it all, she re-focused on bending and molding Brutus to her will to use him as an escape path.

"Brutus," she whispered.

Brutus stopped sucking and Shanea huffed. She had to interrupt him because she couldn't be the one in the trap, it had to be him. "Did…did…you…hear something?" Brutus asked in an octave higher than normal.

Shanea snickered. "No, I want to please you. Let me down."

"Huh?" Brutus asked as he slowly rolled her out to the side which most men could never do and looked at her.

Shanea grinned and then turned her index finger upside down, bouncing it, pointing at his crotch. "No time for romance. Let me suck and fuck this fat thing."

Brutus grinned ear to ear with a school kid-like enthusiasm. He lowered her gently to the ground and Shanea stared up at him the whole way down to her knees. She scrunched her towel up to pad her knees and ran both palms up his thick thighs, then across his black belt holding his nightstick and keys. Her eyes filtered to his member as it strained against the fabric at eye level.

She licked her lips then made eye contact with him again and leaned over to it as she started unbuckling his belt. Shanea stuck her tongue out flat, sliding further back onto her heels to start at the tip which made her giggle. She moaned as she moved up the fabric, the smell of his starched pants flooding her nostrils. It took several long seconds to reach the top as it crossed over into his crotch.

"This is soooo fat…" Shanea moaned.

Brutus chuckled and then groaned as Shanea took his zipper in between her teeth and started to tug it down, eyes up from below locked on his. When she finally made it to the bottom, the clink of his belt being undone, and his pants being unbuttoned made Brutus' member throb next to her ear. Shanea slowly moved her fingers up his waistline and tugged them over his long shaft which bounced up and down in front of her like a springboard.

Shanea gasped and then immediately went to work. Time, she knew, was of the essence. It was only a matter of minutes. She would have to fuck him later. Get him on the hook, then take him down. Twisting both wrists and sucking as hard and as fast as she could, Shanea had him on the ropes in just a few moments, his grunts and groans from above turning her on. She heard him grunting over her and went faster and harder, her jaw starting to ache from the effort.

"Shanea," he hissed, attempting to pull back. "I'ma cum,

and I don't want to cum in your mouth." Shanea yelped as Brutus yanked her to her feet and spun her around. "Up against the wall."

Shanea laughed and then hurried to the wall and placed her palms flat against it. She glanced over her shoulder and watched Brutus approach, biting her bottom lip and gnawing it as she stared at his member bouncing as he walked over to her. He snatched it by the base of the shaft and slid it right between her legs, sliding it across her lips like a saw as he made sure she was ready for him and his girth.

"Hmmmm," Shanea moaned as she slid her ass to his pelvis and bumped it a few times with loud smacks of skin as she stared into his eyes over her shoulder. "You betta *not* go easy on me."

Brutus chuckled. "You may——-"

Brutus stopped and hissed as Shanea quickly slid her hand under her and lined him up, then arched her back as far as it would go and placed him at her hot wet opening.

"Bring…it," Shanea moaned as she twerked, her lower back screaming at her to go back to normal.

Brutus slid his hands to her hips as his eyes stayed glued on her cheeks as they collided on his abs. He slowly slid the tip past her lips and Shanea's eyes bulged as she exhaled a harsh breath. "Sorry," Brutus grunted as he pushed the tip in.

"Don't worry——-" Shanea growled as she let her arch go and started to slide up his shaft with effort as her walls stretched wider than they ever had. "I…I…" She rapidly tapped her palm on the wall with a whimper. "I can take it," she said an octave higher.

Brutus chuckled and shook his head as Shanea started to slide toward the tip, then back, then forward again as she took his member. Brutus grunted when they caught a rhythm. The pair grunted, groaned, and moaned as their skin slapped.

Shanea reached behind her and stuck her hand back. Brutus snatched it and arched her back. "Fuck!" Shanea moaned as Brutus went balls deep. "That big!"

Brutus laughed and then started to fuck her harder and faster. He let Shanea go who turned back around and placed both palms, ear flat to the wall as Brutus smashed her. The pair continued to grunt, and Shanea was getting close. She came on Brutus' dick as silently as she could, her body shaking and shivering as she bit her lip as hard as she could. Brutus wasn't far behind her as she felt him tense.

"Come in me," Shanea gasped as she gripped him as hard as she could.

Brutus grunted and then let loose with an animalistic growl. The python between his legs shot so much seed that it leaked out past his shaft as he continued to jackhammer her. She took deep inhales and exhales of breath, her chin dropping to her chest until Brutus finally slid his spent member from her and tucked it back in his pants.

Shanea turned around with a weary smile, placed her hands in his and smiled up at him. "So, when we have more time." She rubbed the tips of his fingers with her own. "You think we can sneak off somewhere else and have a bit more fun?"

Brutus smirked as he fastened his belt. "Yeah, but we have to pick the time and the place." He cleared his throat. "I'll… uh, I'll be behind the wall while you dress."

Shanea winked and blew him a kiss as he turned around. As he walked away, she saw the carabiner swaying on his hip like Gibbs had. Option number two was for him to walk her straight out the front door like she had watched on the news recently. Seemed easy enough.

Chapter 8

After their encounter and reality set in the next day, Shanea knew that her key plan wasn't going to work. There were just too many unknown variables. So, day in and day out, Shanea Rollins worked in the laundry as her first several months passed. The hope of making a break the first week was unrealistic she realized once she figured out her daily routine. The keys were going to be another impossibility unless she could get her hands on something that would incapacitate the warden, Gibbs, and Brutus all in one shot, and that wouldn't happen. And hurting Brutus was the furthest thing from her mind.

The day after Shanea had Brutus, she started in the laundry and sweated out her hair and had to peel her uniform off from the steam, and it had been like that every day since, six days a week, twelve hours a day. With a lonely Thanksgiving and the most despairing Christmas that had her bawling her eyes out passed along with her work schedule. But every night, Brutus would lock her in the cell with a smile, protective of her when any other prisoner passed. There had been no gen pop for her. The warden made sure of that as long as she kept his member drained which she did twice a week.

Shanea had clocked every single movement of Gibbs which was hard to do because she never had a set pattern, then the warden and when he went home for the day. She had him clocked first as he would leave after she finished blowing him to make it home for dinner. The last piece of the puzzle was Brutus who worked the guard tower closest to the front gate every Friday night, the rest of the time he was on the wing seldom going home, and a newer female guard took his place that night who basically ignored her. Brutus and Shanea had sex every Wednesday night after lights out and with the dick he had, he put her lights out so well that she was sore the next day as she stood doing laundry.

Gibbs had left her alone for the most part after she got her taste. Only demanding it every other Friday night when Brutus was in the guard tower so there wouldn't be any witness on her side, although the prisoners on her wing knew but they kept quiet. The no-snitching rule was very serious at Belmont as death was the usual penalty for it.

The only surety of Gibbs' schedule was every day at three-thirty, she would walk past the laundry, and lick her lips as she eyed Shanea, and then continue on with her day. Shanea had plotted day after day and after the first several weeks, she had a plan. A few weeks prior, after the pair finished and Gibbs was getting dressed, she realized for the first time that Gibbs' clothes could fit her. If she could get the warden and her alone in his office on a Friday night when Brutus was manning the guard tower, she was going to knock her and the warden out, strip Gibbs of her uniform, take both keys to her freedom, and then simply stroll out the front door. Brutus may not even catch on if she wore Gibbs' lieutenant hat.

As the morning of breakout week approached, Thursday, the day before D-Day, Friday, February fourteenth, Valentine's Day to be exact for the break, she was ready for the do-or-die moment. The plan was to get Gibbs ready and primed, have her talk to the warden about a threesome, and then finish the game. Shanea scrubbed her teeth, staring at herself in the mirror. She had discarded the paper clips as they would be no help and the risk was too high for the random cell searches. But she was proud of herself that she did start her plan off by any means necessary.

She heard a knock of a baton on her door and Brutus say, "Ms. Rollins, it's time for work."

Shanea spit into the sink and shook her head with a chuckle as she splashed water into her mouth to clean the excess out before spitting into the sink again as the door opened and Brutus stood in the doorway, blocking the light of the hallway out.

"Morning, Brutus," Shanea said as she slipped into her green loafers.

"Ms. Rollins," Brutus said with a nod.

To keep up appearances there were absolutely no flirtations between the two of them in the slightest. As she walked over to the door, Brutus turned his wide neck in both directions like he always did to check for any danger and when none was present, he stepped back and let her walk out. Twenty-seven paces was the extent of her world and workout. She refused to go outside and stare up at a sun she would never again see without a cage over her head. She could pace her room and that's what she did. So, twenty-seven paces from her door to the laundry, then another twenty to her station at the far back.

"See ya later, Brutus," Shanea said as she entered the steam-filled room.

"Ms. Rollins," Brutus said and then continued.

Shanea walked to her station and gave a head nod to a few of the other women whom she didn't speak to. The lead supervisor, a female guard with short silver hair who Shanea called Butchy, eyed her up and down and then went back to scanning the other prisoners. Shanea huffed as she approached her station, flicked the steamer on and picked up a piece of laundry to start her shift. Hour after hour passed and Shanea pressed and folded like she always did.

And just about the end of her shift, Shanea heard Gibbs shout, "Inmate Rollins!"

Shanea stuck her head out beside her station and shouted, "Yeah?"

"To the front."

Shanea growled and then flicked her steamer off. "What does that heffa want?" Shanea grumbled as she dried her hands off with a rag she kept beside her and then walked to the front.

Gibbs stood with her arms crossed waiting. Shanea approached cautiously and Gibbs's finger waved her forward as she pulled a pair of handcuffs from her belt. Shanea sighed and extended her hands, glaring at Gibbs as she closed the cuffs a little too tight.

Shanea winced and then asked, "Where to?"

"Warden's office, you know the drill," Gibbs said, pushing her by the shoulder in the direction of the office.

Shanea knew the way. But Thursdays weren't usually days she saw the warden so this was new and as she walked, she grinned quickly so Gibbs wouldn't see her. A final scouting opportunity before the Friday night break if she could get both of them to be there. The pair didn't speak as they walked down the hallway. And after months of being on the inside, the gen pop women stopped harassing her. And the one who attacked her had an accident and fell down a flight of stairs... twice, courtesy of Brutus.

Brutus knew what was happening and she felt a strong connection to him, and she would avert her eyes whenever she came back, and he was working her hall. Shanea was embarrassed by what she was being forced to do. The one thing that kept her going was the million in the woods and a nice warm spot on a beach in Cuba with no extradition laws. She had plenty of contacts in Florida who imported cigars and drugs and could smuggle her out on a boat if she could get the escape pulled off.

The pair walked through both doors and then into the entrance to the warden's office. His secretary had checked out for the day, a kind older woman who smiled at Shanea every time she saw her. It wasn't a lustful smile, just a kind grandmotherly smile that made Shanea feel just a little better when she did see her. There wasn't much to smile about in Belmont and giving her and Brutus a smile made her day seem less dreary.

Shanea stopped in the center where she always did and as she waited for Gibbs to walk around her, she cut her eyes at the coat rack and saw a coat that usually wasn't there. Shanea raised an eyebrow as Gibbs tapped her knuckle on the glazed glass of Warden Linwood Michael's door.

"Come in!" Linwood barked.

Gibbs turned the brass handle and opened it, then stepped aside and Shanea walked through. When she entered, she growled low. In front of her, sitting in one of the plush chairs was the judge who had sentenced her to twenty years. Balding and overweight with beady eyes, just a few pounds less than the warden sat Judge Carl Smith. The pair made eye contact and Shanea glared at him with the most sinister look she could muster.

"What's he doing here?" Shanea spat.

"Oh," Linwood said as he walked around the desk. "My old friend Carl who handed your sentence to me for imprisonment has swung by to say *hello*." He cut his eyes at Gibbs who stood silently behind her. "You can go, Lieutenant."

Gibbs stared at the judge and the warden and then gave a sharp nod. "I'll be outside, Sir."

When Gibbs left, Shanea's eyes moved to the judge. "Fuck…that…piece…of…shit," she hissed as the steam rose from her neck.

Linwood leaned his hefty frame against his desk as he made it in front of it, the wood creaking in protest. He chuckled and then said, "Yeah, that's the idea, convict."

Shanea stared through the warden, her heart thumping with hatred and adrenaline, and then her gaze went to the window where the sun was setting, a lone seagull lazily flying around in circles in front of it as if it had not a care in the world. How good would that view look on the beach in Cuba with a Backwoods in one hand and in the other a Mai Tai?

Shanea stood stunned for a long moment as her eyes went to the judge, the sneer of seething hatred still on her lips. Shanea knew that if she lunged and got even one punch landed on him, she would go to solitary which was a bit worse than protective custody that she had been upgraded to. But it would feel oh so good. And with a prison break on the horizon, she slowly lowered her head and a tear fell from her eye.

Shanea cleared her throat, swallowed the spit gathering in her mouth, and then raised her chin high. "You watching then?"

Linwood laughed and picked up his cell phone. "Watching?" He shook his head with an ear-to-ear grin. "Noooo, I'm filming your whore ass getting spit roasted and posting that shit on a porn channel."

Shanea growled low. How much was freedom worth?

Chapter 9

"**H**ow do you wanna start?" Shanea growled, knowing she was going to do everything she could to make them quick hits to get out of there as fast as possible.

She would do it, but she would make sure the warden paid severely when she came back tomorrow night. This was just a lead-in for the idea to be pitched when he finished. Linwood smirked and pointed to the Persian rug in front of him as Judge Carl Smith rose to his feet and started to loosen his red tie and unbutton his pressed white shirt.

With two power-hungry fat white men in front of her and nowhere to go, Shanea reached for the bottom of her striped shirt and rolled it up her stomach, over her chest, and then pulled her braids through it. Carl wolf whistled when he saw her and Linwood laughed. "That ain't shit, Carl. Wait till you see the bottom half."

Shanea rolled her eyes and then pulled her sports bra off and tossed it to the side. She eyed Carl who yanked his tie off and placed it on the warden's desk as he continued to unbutton his shirt. Linwood gave a nod to her pants and Shanea turned around and slid her thumbs in the sides and lightly tugged it down her ass cheeks and swung her braids at the same time, drawing both men's eyes to it.

"Jesus Christ," Carl hissed as he went hard. "That's perfect."

Linwood laughed as he unbuckled his belt and let it flop to either side of his pants. Shanea smacked one of her cheeks and then pulled the fabric rolled under them to jiggle her caramel flesh. Carl couldn't contain himself as he started to rub his hard-on, eyes wide. It was probably the first time he had seen something that wasn't a pancake. Shanea bent over at the waist and heard the distinct sound of the warden's camera clicking pictures. Shanea suppressed the growl in her throat, rolled her pants to her ankles and stepped out of them.

She stood back up and then turned around with her hands on her hips. "Let's get this over with," she muttered, stepping forward and going to her knees in front of the warden.

Linwood laughed and motioned for Carl to lean against the desk with him. Carl slid over, unbuckled his pants and opened his belt as well. They both unzipped their flies and pulled their members from within. Shanea snickered when she saw Carl's.

If he was three inches, that would have been a stretch. She had seen larger shrimp at Walmart grocery shopping than his.

Shanea leaned forward and started with the warden. As degrading as it may have been, she could leverage and make him order her back the following night if she got him to pop his cork with her head game so he wouldn't get a chance to fuck her. She took Linwood in her mouth, reached a hand over to Carl and started to jerk him off. She did her best to suppress her laugh about Carl's dick as she deepthroated Linwood over and over.

Linwood liked to dominate, and he would make sure to hold her by the back of the neck to his stomach as she choked. Shanea had gotten used to it and was able to breathe through her nose rapidly. She popped off Linwood with a gasp of breath and then coughed and went over to Carl.

As she swallowed him, the thought of biting it off took center stage. But with that would come charges and solitary. So, she slid closer to him and switched up with her hand on Linwood's spit-drenched member to jerk him off.

She swung her arms out wide and pulled both of them closer together with her hands. With them side by side, she started to alternate between them. Groaning and moaning could be heard, but she refused to make eye contact with either the judge or the warden. The only man she made eye contact with in her life was Brutus. She didn't want them to see her hate-filled eyes.

It took less than five minutes for Carl to pop his fork and

she yanked his member out of her mouth and aimed it away from her as he came with a shout on Linwood's Persian rug. She rolled her eyes and went back to Linwood who elbowed Carl and said, "Not on my rug, asshole."

"Sorry," Carl muttered, wiping his brow with his palm before shoving his dick back in his pants. "Best head I've ever had."

The warden took a bit longer than most guys. And she knew he was about to yank her to her knees, slam her over his desk, and shove himself inside her. Shanea grabbed his member with both hands and twisted and jerked him off faster and harder than she ever had. Linwood groaned and pulled his hand from her elbow.

Shanea continued as Carl watched, his hands flat on the desk behind him. "Fuck!" Linwood shouted as his ass came off the table and shot his load into Shanea's mouth who swallowed it down.

Linwood slid his arms back and placed his palms on the desk like Linwood with a satisfied sigh. Shanea waited a moment and looked up at him as he rolled his neck back and his chest heaved. When he looked down at her, he said, "Usually, you let me fuck you."

Shanea shrugged as she stood up and went to put her clothes on. "I love our Friday nights."

Linwood raised an eyebrow. "Really?"

Shanea shimmed her pants up her body and looked him

dead in the eye. "I guess I like being submissive to a man in power."

Linwood nudged Carl with a smirk. "See the power I hold?"

"Wish I was that lucky," Carl muttered.

Shanea pulled her sports bra on and then her shirt, pulled her box braids through and dropped them behind her after fluffing them out. "So, we on for tomorrow?" Shanea asked.

Linwood grinned with a nod. "Oh, yeah."

"Can Lieutenant Gibbs be there too?" she asked as she headed for the door.

"Gibbs!" Linwood shouted.

Gibbs opened the door and stepped in. "Sir?"

"It's you, me, and the convict tomorrow night."

Gibbs glared at Shanea who smiled as she walked past her and into the foyer. Her heart thumped in her chest as she waited for Gibbs to answer who was silent for a long moment. As Shanea reached the next door and waited for Gibbs to open it and escort her down the hall, Shanea heard her say, "I'm off tomorrow night, warden for my date with my husband, remember?"

"I care?" Linwood said. "You work for me."

Gibbs cleared her throat, her skin flushing as she did, and then said, "Okay, I'll be here."

An ear-to-ear grin crossed Shanea's lips. She changed her look as Gibbs closed the warden's door and walked over to her, yanking the next one open without a word but with a harsh glare. Shanea stepped through and started to walk down the hallway, ignoring the look. As the pair walked, Shanea kept her eyes straight ahead. The threesome had only happened one other time and it seemed to Shanea that Gibbs got extremely jealous when she watched the warden have his way with her. Shanea could feel the energy in the room as the warden pounded away. There could only ever be one alpha in a room.

"What are you trying to pull, convict?" Gibbs growled as they made it halfway down the hallway.

Shanea shrugged. "I'm not sure what you mean."

Gibbs slid her baton from the holster and moved it up to Shanea's shoulder and pushed until Shanea stopped and faced her. "You're up to something."

"Nah," Shanea said as her heart thumped in her chest on the off-chance Gibbs had figured it out. "I just want to have fun on Valentine's Day."

Gibbs smirked and then lowered her baton. "Is that right?"

Shanea turned and started walking. "Yeah, I know I'm going to spend the next twenty of them in here and I am just setting traditions to make it easier to do my time." She shrugged again. "I like routines and something to look forward to."

Gibbs clicked her tongue as the pair reached her door. She unlocked it and Shanea walked in, "Okay, I'll see you tomorrow night, convict."

Chapter 10

A few hours later after the lights-out call had been given, Shanea heard a knock on her door, rousing her from her slumber. "Yeah?" Shanea croaked.

"It's Brutus, can I come in?" he asked.

Brutus was always polite and never barged into her cell. Other inmates weren't so lucky, especially the ones who threw shit or piss at him when he walked by. Shanea had seen him club a few of them hard enough to break bones and send them to a hospital. It's a dangerous place and to keep law and order with some of the women, he had to do what he had to do.

"Yea, c'mon in," Shanea said as she cleared her throat.

Her door swung open, and Brutus walked in. He closed the door so only a sliver of light shined through and walked over to Shanea who sat up. He didn't say anything as he sat on the end of the bed. Shanea saw the look he had and asked, "Everything okay, Brutus?"

Brutus sniffed and shrugged. "It's the tenth anniversary of my wife's death."

Shanea's jaw dropped before she quickly recovered. "I'm sorry, Brutus."

Brutus turned his head in her direction and gave a sad smile. "Thanks." He paused. "Ya know, I'm starting to care about you and enjoy our time together----"

Shanea cleared her throat when he stopped abruptly, not sure whether to say what was on his mind. "And?" she asked.

Brutus sighed and rubbed his palm over his face. "I'm retiring next week. I'm getting too old for this shit."

Shanea gasped. She knew it would happen and she felt horrible and sick to her stomach that she wouldn't be able to tell of her escape plans. He would have to stop her. But with him retiring and if tomorrow was a bust and she was sentenced to more time, there would be no one to protect her from whatever waited for her the following morning. Shanea had picked the night because of his tower duty. It was one thing to stop her but shoot her, he couldn't do it, he wouldn't do it. At least Shanea was sure to believe he wouldn't.

"What am I going to do now?" Shanea muttered as her head dropped.

Brutus moved his hand over to her chin and lifted it as he leaned in and silently kissed her softly. The pair locked lips, quiet and soft, long and sensual. Shanea ran her palm over his cheek as Brutus moved both hands to hers. Shanea slid a little closer and when the kiss broke, she buried her head into his shoulder and started to cry. This was as much closure as she was going to get.

They were quiet for several minutes, Shanea's sobs muffled by Brutus' shirt, the dripping water from her faucet their only accompaniment. Finally, Shanea pulled back with a loud sniff and the pair locked eyes, Brutus' soft and caring, hers timid. She could feel the pain he felt at leaving. It wasn't about the sex, each of them found comfort in the other and that was being snuffed out.

"So, what now?" Shanea asked, softly.

Brutus lowered his head and shook it. "Not sure."

"Will you write me under a different name?" Shanea asked.

Brutus cleared his throat. "I can do that."

Shanea couldn't tell him the plan, but she could drop a hint and if he could figure it out, he could come looking for her when he retired. "You know the one thing I regret the most?"

Brutus leaned his head back. "What's that?"

Shanea sniffed and said, "I always wanted to move to Cuba, and I could have with all the money I had…" She paused. "If I had, I wouldn't be here now, would I? I think when I get parole that's exactly where I'm gonna go."

"Well, when that day comes, I'll carry your bags when I meet you at the front gate."

Shanea smiled and then kissed him softly again. Her hands

slowly moved up his chest as their kiss became more passionate. Brutus slid his hands under Shanea's shirt, rolled her bra over her breasts, and squeezed them, causing Shanea to moan in their kiss. She slid one of her palms over his thigh and squeezed his hardening member. Shanea pressed her palm against his chest and Brutus froze as their lips broke apart.

"Is something wrong?" he asked.

Shanea gave him a wicked grin and leaned back, letting his hands fall from her. She rolled her shirt over her head and tossed it on the floor. She slid back and then lay back on the bed, lifting her ass and tugging her pants off as she kept her eyes locked on his. She threw them at Brutus playfully who chuckled as he watched her roll over onto her stomach and seductively get on her hands and knees, back arched as far as it could to pop her ass out.

Brutus moaned and gnawed his lip when he saw her. Shanea winked and silently crawled over to him and leaned down to his thigh to lick a line of saliva along his imprint which made him moan. Shanea grabbed one of his hands and yanked it back to her ass with a giggle. Brutus' hands were so large that they covered half her large ass cheek with no problem. He spread his fingers wide and kneaded the caramel flesh.

Shanea slid both hands to his belt and yanked it apart. Brutus lifted slightly, his stomach muscles bunching as she unbuttoned them and tugged them down. Brutus lifted his hand and smacked her ass cheek which made a loud clap that made them both look at the door and then laugh. No one would come down the hallway as it was in the middle of the night and the other prisoners were asleep.

Shanea rolled his boxers over his shaft, and it popped up, springing side to side like a pendulum. Shanea licked her lips and drove her lips right over the tip and then down the shaft as Brutus groaned above her. She snatched his free hand and moved it onto the top of her head as his other hand gripped her ass cheek as hard as he could, making her wet. Shanea wedged as much of his member down her throat as she could as she choked and gagged.

"I'm going to miss this," Brutus gasped as he bobbed her head up and down.

Shanea laughed as she sucked and then refocused. She would miss it, too. She started to go faster and harder, using both hands to get his toes to curl in his shiny black shoes. Brutus slid his hand down and gently lifted her by the stomach which made her groan in protest, but she knew what he wanted. His favorite position and hers as well with his large member was her on top bouncing until the squeaky bed sounded like it was going to snap into a million pieces.

"Oh, Daddy wants me to bounce, huh?" Shanea said with a giggle as she straddled him and looked up from below as he still towered over her.

Brutus grinned with a nod as Shanea slid her hand under her and guided him to her opening. She rubbed it back and forth several times, wetting the tip, and then lifted a bit to slide him inside her. The first stroke was always the hardest as it took the wind from her lungs when she exhaled loudly from the stretch, but over the months she had become accustomed to it. As he entered her, Shanea leaned against his barrel chest and exhaled a loud whoosh of air.

"Jesus," she groaned as she inched her way down his wide shaft. "That's thick."

"You say that every time," Brutus said with a chuckle.

Shanea swung both arms around his chest in a bear hug and started to grind back and forth, her ear pressed to his heart as she did. Brutus wrapped his arms around her the same way and pulled her in tighter until she felt like she was going to pop. Shanea started to lift and slam down, their skin slapping making her ready to feel every inch of him on every thrust. Up and down she went, repeatedly. As she rode, a single tear fell from her eye, but she continued. This would be the final time, no matter how much she didn't want it to be.

The pair caught a rhythm and Brutus slid his wide hands to her hips and gripped them tight, his fingertips digging into her flesh. Shanea bounced harder, making it to the balls of her feet before swinging her leg around and moving to reverse cowgirl without missing a beat. Shanea continued to bounce, sliding her hands to her knees, keeping up a continuous rhythm.

She could hear Brutus' breathing increase and knew he was on the ropes. Every time he had pulled out, she held her breath, wanting to remember this night forever. She knew she would escape…she had to escape. As Brutus went to pull her off, she hooked her hands under his knees when she felt his member pulsate and waited as her ass cheeks clapped his thighs.

"Shanea," Brutus hissed. "Let me pull-------"

"No," Shanea barked. "Give…it…to…me."

Brutus' body spasmed as he came. Shanea held on as she felt his hot seed shoot into her. Once he finished, Brutus leaned his head forward as the sweat dripped from his chin and onto her lower back. The pair stayed that way for a long time until Shanea slowly lifted up and turned around.

She leaned over at the waist, wrapped both hands around Brutus' neck and nuzzled his forehead before pecking it. "One day, hopefully before I'm too old, I'll get to a beach near Havana."

Brutus smiled as he stared at his knees. "You can do anything you put your mind to, of that, I have no doubt."

Chapter 11

Friday morning came faster than expected. The soft pink light from the rising sun warmed her eyelids and face. Shanea yawned and blinked the sleep from her eyes and then winced when she moved. Her pussy was sore like it was every time. But on that morning, it felt different, she felt whole. She would miss Brutus more than she thought she would.

Shanea slowly made it to her elbow and yawned a second time. She swung her legs over the edge of the bed and made it to her feet with a wince. She checked the wall clock. 7:00 am. Shanea walked over to her sink and started her day. She looked in the mirror as she brushed her teeth, her heart pumping so hard and fast that she felt like she was having a heart attack. In twelve hours, she would be walking down the main line in Gibbs' uniform, out the front door, and into the night.

As she washed her face in the sink, she thought of every tiny detail she could. Work until five, get ready and primed for the Friday night festivities, and then make a break for it. She had studied Gibbs' body for any weaknesses over the last few months and found one small flaw in an otherwise well-built physique. Gibbs had a bad habit of leaning to the right when she escorted Shanea down hallways which meant some type of hip problem and if they had to fight, Shanea would hit that hip first before a hard right hook she had.

There was a knock on the door and the guard who worked Brutus' shift while he manned the tower said, "Rollins, let's go."

"Okay," Shanea shouted back as she slid her green loafers on and walked to the door.

The door swung open, and the guard stepped aside. Shanea didn't even acknowledge her as she took the twenty-seven paces to the laundry that was just kicking off. Shanea walked in and then back to her station without a word to the other women like she did every other day of the week. Shanea steamed the clothes for her whole shift, her heart thumping every second of every minute of every hour. She couldn't keep her eyes off the clock. Shanea went to lunch, and came back to the steamer, then as the workday came to an end, Shanea shut her machine down and waited for her escort back to the cell.

No other prisoners were given the luxury, just her. As long

as the warden stayed fulfilled, she would be protected. The same guard who walked her in led her back to her cell and opened the door. When the pair made eye contact, the guard said, "You know the deal, Rollins."

Shanea smirked and said, "Yeah, I know the deal."

The code for be ready at seven to serve the warden's every desire. Shanea had gotten used to it over the months and went to work prepping as usual. She waited for an hour and the guard came back and led her to the showers. Shanea had the showers down to a science. It took exactly three minutes to warm up and four to wash clean before the water turned cold again. Seven whole minutes.

Once she was back in her cell, she lifted her mattress and pulled out her outfit that the warden had her wear on the nights she went there. The schoolgirl outfit was a bit much but what else could she expect from a power-hungry overweight sadistic white man? She slid the low-cut top on, then the short cut frilly skirt. She looked herself over in the mirror and adjusted her breasts and then picked up a fresh striped shirt and pants, pulling them over the outfit.

"Guard," Shanea said as she fluffed her braids. "I'm ready."

6:55…

The door creaked open, and Shanea walked out into the hallway. The perspiration poured from her underarms and down her ass crack as her lower back sweated. This particular guard always walked a step behind her, and she wasn't entirely sure why. In all fairness, Shanea was known to be a violent inmate who the warden didn't think needed to be shackled any longer. As the pair walked down the silent hallway, the clack from the guard's spit-shined black shoes was deafening in her ears. There wasn't a sound anywhere that she didn't hear as she walked.

The pair made it to the foyer of the warden's office and the guard walked past her to knock on the door. The guard tapped her knuckle on the door and Linwood shouted, "Send her in."

Shanea took a deep breath as the guard opened the door and stepped aside. Shanea exhaled a deep breath and walked forward. Her legs felt like she had steel weights attached to her ankles, and as she walked, she almost collapsed several times as her adrenaline started to overtake her.

Shanea clenched her fists open and closed as she walked to try and dissipate some of the energy. As she crossed into the room, Linwood was behind the desk and Gibbs was nowhere to be seen. Shanea's heart sank to the deepest parts of her stomach. All that work for nothing.

"Convict," Linwood said as he acknowledged her. "Come and sit down."

Shanea cleared her throat and did her best to control her breathing. It felt like she could feel every breath pounding in her ears as she walked. Shanea made it to the chair and sat down.

"Where is Gibbs?" she asked.

Linwood looked up from his papers and shrugged. "If she

isn't looking to get fired, she better be here in the next few minutes."

Shanea gave a sharp nod. She clenched the fabric on her thighs and kneaded it. Linwood looked at her hands and asked, "Something wrong, convict?"

Convict…never her name as if she were just a number. Shanea growled low and then shook her head. "Nah," she said. "Just looking to get that good dick you give me."

Linwood grinned. The snare had been set. Now, all she needed was Gibbs and his balls emptied and she was ready to go. Linwood stood up and checked his phone. He opened it when it dinged and read the message. He smirked and then held his hand up and started to countdown.

Five, four, three, two, one…

He pointed at the door, and it opened. Gibbs stood in the doorway, swaying slightly, a duffel bag in her hand, a bottle in the other. Linwood arched a brow and Shanea couldn't help but snicker. Then it dawned on her that she was fucked. Gibbs was wearing her regular clothes…of all the shitty luck. Shanea's heart dropped again.

"Are you drunk, Gibbs?" Linwood shouted as the guard by the door laughed and then covered her mouth.

Gibbs held up her index finger and thumb and slurred as she strolled in, "Only a tiny bit."

"Guard," Linwood snapped.

"Sir?"

"You may leave."

"Yes, Sir," the guard said, then snickered at Gibbs.

It was out of character for Gibbs to be drunk. She was too controlled for that. Shanea watched her close the door, walk over to the couch and drop the duffel bag on it as she plopped down beside it.

"Gibbs," Linwood snarled.

Gibbs' head lolled side to side with a shit-eating grin. She hiccupped and said, "Yeah?"

"You better have a fucking good excuse as to why you are like this," he shouted, pointing a meaty index finger at her.

Gibbs shrugged. "My husband wasn't happy that I had to cut our evening short and said I should have one at least." She held the bottle up and shook it. "Had a little more than one. I don't like seeing you without clothes on."

Shanea looked at Linwood who was seething. His hands shook as he stared her down. "I should fire you right now!" he roared.

Gibbs blew a raspberry and said, "You do that, and I'll let everyone know that little Blaine is yours. Your wife ain't gonna like that is she?"

"Blaine?" Shanea mouthed.

Linwood stood frozen, the vein in the center of his forehead throbbed. "You wouldn't dare," he hissed.

Gibbs smirked. "I should go to the papers, shouldn't I? Your job should be mine, Linwood. You stole it."

had seen enough fights break out to know to slide back. She started to edge the chair back. The date of escape was going to be pushed back, there was no doubt about that. This was some crazy baby momma drama that was about to pop off. Of all the luck. A plan to get them both in the same room just blew up in her face.

She spoke up, "Ummm, looks like y'all have some serious shit to work out. I'll…" She stood up. "I'll head back to the cell."

"Sit…down," Linwood roared.

Shanea sat back down and slid a little further back as Linwood approached Gibbs who straightened up. Linwood towered over her and glared down at her. "I always looked out for you, Gibbs," he snarled. "And the night I want you two at the same time one more time, you pull this shit! And threaten to tell the papers that your kid is my kid?"

"I don't like you fucking my ho," Gibbs hissed with a coldness that was in character but a little misplaced. "You greedy fuck."

"Wait a minute," Shanea shouted. "Who you callin' a ho?"

Gibbs and Linwood ignored her, they were too focused on one another. Shanea watched as it unfolded, and her eyes cut to the slightly open gym bag. Shanea cocked her head to the side and smiled. Gibbs had her uniform in there. She was planning on spending the night. It could still work. Maybe they would kill each other.

The pair continued to stare each other down and finally, Gibbs made it to her feet and swayed slightly. Linwood, as large as he was, moved much faster than Shanea or Gibbs expected him to. He had his hands around her neck so fast that Gibbs stumbled back onto the couch, the bottle still in her hand, Linwood on top of her. Shanea sat dumbfounded as the two traded blows with one another. She looked at the gym bag, then the door, back to the gym bag as the pair of them fought.

Shanea heard Gibbs choking and watched as Linwood applied more pressure. Gibbs brought both arms down inside his and loosened his grip. She took a deep breath of air and then smashed her bottle across his head, sending him rolling to the side as the blood splattered over the seat cushions. Gibbs sat up with a huge gulp of air and then stood up. She started to kick Linwood in the side, her boot crunching his ribs after every shot as he reached for his ankle.

Shanea slid over to the desk, grabbed Linwood's letter opener and held it behind her back. Either way, Shanea knew the code; as a witness, she knew two people could keep a secret if one of them was dead. She looked at the letter opener and then the lamp next to her. With Gibbs' back turned, she knew to make her move.

Chapter 12

Shanea yanked the cord from the wall and stood up. She let Gibbs land two more blows and then she rushed over and smashed the lamp over Gibbs' head, knocking her unconscious. Gibbs pitched forward and fell over Linwood. Linwood's head lolled to the side, the blood seeping from his head wound. The pair made eye contact and then his eyes rolled back in his head and his chest stopped moving.

"Oh fuck!" Shanea shouted as she rushed over.

She placed her ear on Linwood's chest and waited for a heartbeat…nothing. She pressed her fingers to his jugular and found a weak pulse. He was alive but for how long she didn't know. The one thing she did know was that if anyone came in, she was going to get the blame no matter how it happened. A convict's word would never be taken. Shanea looked at the gym bag and then the door.

She stood up and rushed over to it as she yanked her prison uniform off, then the schoolgirl outfit. She tossed everything on the warden's desk and ripped the duffel bag open. She searched madly for the pants, fingers shaking. She found them and pulled them up to her waist, then yanked Gibbs' shirt on. Shanea buttoned it and then pulled her cap from within and tossed the bag on the couch. Her fingers shook uncontrollably as she buttoned the last button at the throat and shoved it in her pants.

Shanea looked at Gibbs and Linwood and then at the door. She saw Linwood's chest rise and fall softly and exhaled a sigh of relief. If she was caught, the most they could pin on her was assault. Another ten years but it beat the chair. She looked over at the warden's desk and saw his water bottle. She smirked and then walked over to it and snatched it, unscrewing the cap and then taking a long pull.

She walked over and knelt next to him and rolled his pockets, yanking his keys and wallet out and flipping through it. He had a few hundred in twenties. Shanea pulled the crisp bills out and shoved them in her pocket. She picked the water bottle up, took another pull, and then tossed the wallet on his chest.

She swished the water around in her mouth and then spat it in the warden's face. He woke with a start and then groaned as he blinked his eyes. When the pair made eye contact, Shanea snatched him by the shirt and yanked him up.

"Yo, warden…" She shook him violently. "Happy Valentine's Day. Appreciate you being greedy," she snarled, then headbutted him, smashing his nose, and knocking him back out.

Shanea hurried to Gibbs' side, dug in her pockets as well and found her keys. With a turn of her heels, she yanked Gibb's shoes off and kicked her loafers off. She laughed as she stood up, wedging her feet in the shiny black shoes, and said, "Glad you a jealous ho."

Shanea shoved everything in her pockets and ran for the door and out into the foyer. She adjusted everything as she reached the next door, her hands violently shaking this time. She yanked open both doors and walked as quickly down the halls as she could.

She didn't see anyone as she walked to the exit. Shanea looked around and over her shoulder twice before she pulled the sets from her pockets and flipped through them. She tried several that didn't work and then tried the third key and it unlocked. Her heart skipped a beat when she heard the deadbolt to freedom click.

She rushed through and threw the keys to the side and moved on to the next door. She started flipping keys as she made it to that door and then found the one she needed. Shanea inserted it into the lock and turned it with her breath caught in her throat. With a simple click, the door unlocked. Shanea froze. In front of her on a dimly lit concrete path was the walkway to her salvation. The longest fifty yards with the most intimidating sight of humongous watch towers looming overhead.

"C'mon, girl, you got this," Shanea growled before stepping onto the concrete.

Footstep after footstep, Shanea Rollins, known to the world as Lady Blaze walked as straight as she could toward the gate. She cut her eyes at the towers and after twenty yards, she saw an officer above her with their rifle posted on their hip. Step after step, she continued. As she reached the gate, she waved to the guard above with her hat titled just right to stop the guard from seeing her full face. As the door creaked open, Shanea heard an all too familiar booming voice.

"Rollins!" It was the Warden's nephew. "Stop!"

Shanea glanced over her shoulder and then sprinted toward the door and freedom as the emergency bell rang out, deafening her. And as she reached the entrance, a lone single shot rang out.

Epilogue

Shanea made her way through the woods to the cacophony of sounds of baying hounds as the alarm blared. Having almost been shot, her heart was racing as she literally ran for her life. The dogs tracked her every move and she got lucky, really lucky. As the baying dogs chased her, she started sprinting down a gravel road in the pitch of night as a car appeared behind her, the dust swirling as it sped down the lane.

As the pair of headlights bore down on her, she sprinted harder and faster, then glanced over her shoulder and tripped. The car came to a screeching halt, splashing gravel in every direction, and when she raised her head at the door that opened, she almost passed out. Brutus held the door open, and she jumped in as he pulled off, leaving the others in the dust.

The first place the pair stopped was the woods that were near her old place to collect her million. Brutus had convinced her to stay in the car and she had let him go. There was only one man she now trusted and that was him. Of course, he could have killed her, should have killed her but they had broken the cardinal rule: Never love a convict and never love a screw.

Brutus drove down to the Florida Panhandle and found a Cuban cigar smuggler. He negotiated the fare and helped Shanea board. They kissed one another goodbye with the promise they would see each other again, but Brutus needed to sew a few last things up.

He went back to work and the days dragged on and on that final month before retirement with Shanea on his mind the entire time. When he got back, he had been told that Warden Linwood Michaels and Lieutenant Gibbs were under arrest.

Apparently, when they woke up, the investigators found them and when they were questioned the truth came out. As a parting gift, Brutus accidentally dropped a ledger that detailed all the dealings that had been happening into the mail to the newspaper to pile more incriminating information onto what they told.

WHEN THE STORY broke on his last day of work and he punched the clock for the last time, the evening news was on. He watched the warden and lieutenant being led from the courthouse in leg irons. With a smirk, he tipped his hat to the men behind the counter and walked out.

A week later, Brutus walked along a narrow path, whistling Earth, Wind, and Fire's, *Sing A Song*, running his beefy hand along the shrubbery as he did. The trunks he wore were tighter than they should have been, but retirement had its benefits.

Brutus walked out onto the sand and dug his toes in with a sigh. He started to walk to his chair overlooking the ocean, the breeze blowing his unbuttoned shirt wide. He walked around and looked down at Shanea with a grin. She beamed back and lowered her sunglasses over the bridge of her nose with a wink as he handed her the Mai Tai in his hand, the glass sweating in the heat.

"You're right, I love you and this country," he said as he sat down.

Shanea took a polite sip and slid her hand into his, intertwining their fingers. "Yeah, Cuba is the spot to retire, huh?"

THE END

Did you enjoy the read?
Let us know how much by leaving us a review on Amazon and Goodreads.

. . .

Keep reading for a preview of...

Wet Dreams On Lockdown: The Librarian

By Ashley Williams

CHAPTER 1

A nigga was tired of the same shit on a day-to-day basis, but hell, what could I expect? For the last 15 years, a nigga was the property of the Mississippi Department of Corrections, known as inmate #0654321. Yep, I went from being a free man to property of this fucked up state, all because I let my temper get the best of me.

I was caught on my charge of manslaughter on March 4th, 2008. A nigga was only 25 at the time, and I was in the streets heavy as fuck. Back then, there wasn't shit nobody could tell me because a nigga head was hard as fuck. My people always used to say to me that I didn't believe pig pussy was pork. Truth was, I didn't. Out in the streets, I didn't feel like nobody was fucking with me when it came to money, cars, and, of course, bitches. I had it all, and in the blink of an eye, that shit was all gone.

On March 4th, I kicked it out West in the projects. I didn't come out here often because these niggas out this way didn't fuck with us South Side niggas. The only reason I was even out this way was because of a little bitch that wanted to be on my team. She had been hitting a nigga up all day, begging me to come drop some dick off in her. Since I didn't have shit else to do that night, I decided to go ahead and stop by.

When I pulled up, I saw a few niggas standing outside, trying to see who the fuck was pulling up in the all-black Crown Victoria. Parking, I pulled out my phone and texted the old girl to let her know I was there. She responded and let me know to come inside the apartment.

Before leaving the car, I checked my surroundings to ensure I was good. Even though I felt like I was that nigga, I wasn't trying to take any chances and get caught slacking. With my gun in my waist, I got out of the car and made my way into the apartment.

As she said, I noticed it was slightly open when I reached the door. Entering the apartment, I instantly felt like something was off. For one, it was dark as fuck, and I also noticed that it was empty as fuck. Everything in me told me to turn around and get on down, but my tuff ass decided to stay.

I called out to ole girl to see if she was in the apartment, but I didn't get anything but silence in return.

I felt like something was about to pop off. I turned around and was about to exit the apartment. As I reached for the door handle, I felt a gun being pressed against the back of my head.

What the fuck? I thought to myself. *Ain't no way I let a bitch set me up.*

"Mane, you know what it is," the nigga holding the gun stated.

"Bruh, you're wasting your time with this one. I ain't got shit on me," I let him know.

"You a fucken lie. My homegirl said you were that nigga out South, and I know y'all boys got plenty of money!" the nigga barked, never taking the gun off the back of my head.

I couldn't lie, a nigga was scared as hell. My whole life flashed before my eyes, but I refused to go out like a little bitch behind some pussy.

After going back and forth with the nigga, he dropped the gun and told me to get the fuck out before he changed his mind and shot my ass anyway.

Not wanting to give the nigga a chance to change his mind, I opened the door and took off in a full sprint towards my car.

As soon as I made it to my car, I cranked it up and put that bitch in reverse. I was both pissed off and relieved at the same time. I was pissed because this hoe-ass bitch had set a nigga up, and I was relieved because the nigga let me go with my life.

"If I ever see that hoe again, Imma kill that bitch," I said as I hit the steering wheel, making my way out of the apartment complex.

Before I could make it entirely out, I spotted the bitch that set me up. Without thinking, I put the car in park, jumped out, and ran down on her ass. At that point, I didn't give a fuck that she was out there with her people. I just had to let this bitch know that she had fucked with the wrong one.

"Say bitch, you thought you were gonna set a real nigga up, huh!" I shouted as soon as I got in her personal space. The bitch couldn't say shit because she knew she had fucked up.

Not giving her time to answer me, I reached into my waistband, took my gun out, and instantly shot her in her muthafucken head, then turned around and made it back to my car. I had to get the fuck up out of there because I did that shit out in the open.

I was still pissed, but I felt better that I took care of that hoe. *I bet that bitch won't set anybody else up again*; I thought as I continued to make my way home.

Just thinking about that night made me wish to go back in time and change my actions, but here I was, out of sight and out of mind. I used to spend my days running wild, and now my every move was clocked, and I spent my days going through a fucken routine.

My day began at the crack of dawn when the guards would come through and make us all get up and get ready to go and eat. Before leaving my bed, I would lie there for a few minutes and reflect on the life I had left behind; for some reason, every day for the last 15 years, that was always my first thought of the day.

Breakfast in the prison cafeteria was a hurried affair. We

had to be in and out within 20-25 minutes. The meals were bland, often watery oatmeal or gritty scrambled eggs. As always, I would scarf down my food, all while exchanging nods with my fellow inmates, acknowledging the unspoken camaraderie that had developed among us.

After breakfast, those who had jobs headed off to our work assignment. I was part of a small crew responsible for maintaining the prison grounds. Under the watchful eyes of the guards, we mowed lawns, trimmed hedges, and picked litter. It was grueling work for no pay, but it gave me a sense of purpose and a brief escape from the confines of my cell.

Since we kept things up daily, we were done with our assignments by the time we were set to go to lunch. Lunchtime offered a brief respite from the day's monotony. I usually would sit with a small group of friends, sharing stories and cracking jokes to forget our grim reality momentarily. Also, while in the prison cafeteria, some inmates would trade goods – cigarettes, snacks, or contraband items discreetly passed from one hand to another. I tended to stay away from that. I didn't have the time to owe anybody anything, and I also refused to go through the hassle of getting into it with anybody for owing me something.

In the afternoon, we were granted a few hours of recreation time. We could play basketball, lift weights, or walk around the fenced-in yard. This was one of these moments of physical activity essential for maintaining my sanity and fitness. Working out kept me looking good and helped me release stress if I had anything going on.

I liked to go to the library and chill out for a little while in the evenings. I didn't start getting into books until I got locked up. Being on the streets the way I was didn't allow me time to sit down and enjoy a book. Reading kept me up with what was happening in the world. Yes, I knew that most of it was made up, but I didn't let that stop me from sticking my nose to a good book. Plus, I liked to take books back to my cell and read before sleeping.

Lastly, there was dinner and then lights out. Dinner in the prison cafeteria mirrored breakfast – a rushed affair with uninspiring food.

This was my experience day in and day out for the last 15 years. This was starting to get old, but I had another five years to do the same daily.

CHAPTER 2

The scorching sun beat down on the sprawling prison yard as I trudged along, the weight of the lawnmower resting heavily on my shoulders. I had just finished cutting the grass, and the sweat-drenched my prison uniform. Every step I took felt like a battle against the sweltering heat, but this was my daily routine, and I had grown accustomed to it over the years.

The rhythmic hum of the lawnmower faded into the distance as I approached the maintenance shed. With relief, I sat the machine down and wiped my brow with the back of my hand. The task was done, and I couldn't deny the satisfaction of completing a job, no matter how mundane. It gave me a sense of purpose in this confined world.

After storing away the lawnmower, I returned to my dormitory. The walk felt endless, but I knew a refreshing shower awaited me. The prison was not the most welcoming place, but I had learned to appreciate the small moments of comfort and solitude.

The rusty shower heads in the communal bathroom did little to ease the oppressive heat that permeated the prison walls, but they were a respite from the unforgiving sun outside. As I stood beneath the lukewarm water, I let it wash away the dirt and sweat, if only temporarily. My mind wandered to the evening ahead, and the anticipation of the football game we had planned to watch lifted my spirits.

The cafeteria buzzed with activity as I approached the lunch line. I grabbed a tray and joined the line of inmates shuffling toward the serving counter. The cafeteria staff dished out the usual unappetizing prison fare, and I couldn't help but suppress a grimace as I accepted my tray. It was far from gourmet, but it filled the stomach, and that's all we could hope for here.

Sitting at a crowded table, I joined a group of fellow inmates eagerly discussing the upcoming football game. The New Orleans Saints were playing the Dallas Cowboys, an exciting matchup. Football was a rare escape from the harsh reality of prison, a fleeting connection to the world beyond these walls.

As I dug into my meal, I couldn't help but get caught up in the lively conversation. We analyzed the strengths and weaknesses of each team, debated over who would emerge victorious, and placed friendly wagers that meant nothing in the grand scheme of things but added a layer of excitement to our otherwise monotonous lives.

Once lunch was over, I decided to forego the recreation period. The sun outside had intensified, turning the prison yard into an unforgiving furnace. I was never a fan of the relentless heat, and today's scorching temperatures only reinforced my decision to remain indoors. Instead, I went to the prison library, hoping to pass the time with a good book.

When I entered the library, something caught my eye. It wasn't a book or a familiar face but the librarian. A new woman had taken over the position, and I couldn't help but be taken aback by her beauty. Her dark hair framed her face perfectly, and her eyes held a depth that seemed to invite exploration. She was an enchanting presence amidst the sterile library shelves.

My heart raced as I approached the librarian's desk. I tried to gather my thoughts, knowing that I should introduce myself. After all, there was no harm in making a new acquaintance, especially in a place like this.

"Hey there," I began, sounding casual, "I'm Tesean Carter. I don't think I've seen you around here before."

The librarian looked up from her desk, her eyes meeting mine. For a moment, there was a flicker of surprise in her gaze, and I hoped that maybe I had piqued her interest. She offered a polite but reserved smile.

"I'm Sophie," she replied, her voice soft and measured. "I just started working here a few days ago."

"New in town, huh?" I continued, trying to keep the conversation flowing. "You getting used to this place?"

Sophie nodded, her smile remaining friendly but guarded. "It's quite different from my previous job, but I'm adjusting."

Encouraged by her response, I pressed on. "Well, if you need help with anything or have questions about the inmates, feel free to ask. I've been here for a while and know the ropes."

Sophie's gaze softened, and she seemed to relax slightly. "Thank you, Tesean. I appreciate that."

With newfound confidence, I decided to take a chance and flirt. "You know, I've got some free time now. If you ever want to chat, you can always find me in the library."

Sophie's smile wavered momentarily, and I could sense a hint of unease in her eyes. She cleared her throat and replied, "I appreciate the offer, Tesean, but I must stay focused on my work. It's important to maintain professionalism here."

Her words hit me like a cold shower. I had been flirting, and she had been courteous but clear in her rejection. I felt embarrassed and disappointed, but I also respected her decision. After all, we were in a prison, and boundaries had to be maintained.

"Of course," I said, trying to mask my disappointment with a smile. "I understand. If you ever change your mind, I'll be right here."

Sophie nodded and returned to her work, and I walked

away from the desk, my pride slightly bruised but my respect for her professionalism intact.

As I perused the library shelves, I couldn't help but feel a mixture of emotions. I had been captivated by Sophie's beauty and had mustered the courage to approach her, but I had also learned the importance of respecting boundaries in a place like this. With its rows of books and newfound librarian, the library had taken on a different significance. It was no longer just a place to escape through literature; it was now a reminder of the unattainable beauty beyond the prison walls.

The hours passed slowly as I immersed myself in a book, trying to lose myself in words and escape the confinement of my surroundings. I had almost forgotten about the upcoming football game and the camaraderie that awaited me back in my dorm.

When I left the library, the sun had descended toward the horizon. The prison yard had transformed from a blistering inferno to a slightly more tolerable environment, but I had no regrets about missing recreation time. Instead, I headed straight to the dorm day room, where the atmosphere was excited.

As I approached the table where my fellow inmates had gathered, they enthusiastically greeted me. The anticipation for the game was palpable, and everyone was eager to see their favorite teams compete. I took my seat, and the friendly banter and predictions continued.

The New Orleans Saints and the Dallas Cowboys were

both well-loved in this group, and the rivalry between their fans added to the excitement. The room was filled with voices, each person passionately defending their team's chances and trading good-natured insults.

As the game kicked off on the small television in the corner of the room, I sat back and enjoyed the festivities of the evening.

Available Now On All Platforms.

OTHER BOOKS BY

<u>URBAN AINT DEAD</u>

Tales 4rm Da Dale

The Hottest Summer Ever

Hittin' Licks For The Holidays: Atlanta

Wet Dreams On Lockdown: The Nurse

By **Elijah R. Freeman**

Despite The Odds

By **Juhnell Morgan**

Good Girl Gone Rogue

By **Manny Black**

Hittaz

Hittaz 2

Hittaz 3

Hittaz 4

Coldhearted

By **Lou Garden Price, Sr.**

Charge It To The Game

Charge It To The Game 2

A Summer To Remember With My Hitta

Snatched Up By A Hitta

Santa Sent Me A Real One For Christmas

Wet Dreams on Lockdown: The Unit Manager

By **Nai**

A Setup For Revenge

Wet Dreams On Lockdown: Librarian

By **Ashley Williams**

Ridin' For You

Trickin' on a Heaux for Christmas: A BBW Love Story

Homie Hoppin' For The Holidays

By **Telia Teanna**

The State's Witness

The State's Witness 2

The State's Witness 3

By **Kyiris Ashley**

Stuck In The Trenches

Stuck In The Trenches 2

By **Huff Tha Great**

The Swipe

By **Toōla**

Melted the Heart of a Menace

By P. Wise

Merry Trapmas: Ice & Frost

By **Mia Sky**

Thug Me The Right Way

By **DiamondATL & Nai**

Wet Dreams on Lockdown: The Male C.O

By **Tamyra Griffin**

Wet Dreams On Lockdown: The Counselor

By **Paris Iman**

COMING SOON

Ridin For You, Too
Wet Dreams On Lockdown: The Female C.O
By **Telia Teanna**

A Setup For Revenge 2
By **Ashley Williams**

A Gangsta's Last Kiss
By **Mia Sky**

Pretti & The Beast
Wet Dreams On Lockdown: Lieutenant Grace
By **P. Wise**

Wet Dreams On Lockdown: The Captain
By **TN Jones**

BOOKS BY

URBAN AINT DEAD's C.E.O

<u>Elijah R. Freeman</u>

Triggadale

Triggadale 2

Triggadale 3

Tales 4rm Da Dale

The Hottest Summer Ever

Murda Was The Case

Murda Was The Case 2

Murda Was The Case 3

Hittin' Licks For The Holidays: Atlanta

Wet Dreams On Lockdown: The Nurse

STAY CONNECTED

Follow

Elijah R. Freeman

On Social Media

FB: Elijah R. Freeman

IG: @the_future_of_urban_fiction